Sallie Muirden is a poet and novelist. Her first novel, *Revelations of a Spanish Infanta*, won the 1996 HarperCollins Fiction Prize. Her second novel, *We Too Shall Be Mothers*, was published in 2001. Her collection of poetry, *The Fable of Arachne*, was published in 2009. Sallie lives in Melbourne with her husband and two children.

Also by Sallie Murden

Revelations of a Spanish Infanta

We Too Shall Be Mothers

The Fable of Arachne

A WOMAN of SEVILLE

*A novel of love, ladders
and the unexpected*

Sallie Muirden

FOURTH ESTATE • *London, New York, Sydney* and *Auckland*

Fourth Estate
An imprint of HarperCollins*Publishers*

First published in Australia in 2009
by HarperCollins*Publishers* Australia Pty Ltd
ABN 36 009 913 517
harpercollins.com.au

HarperCollins*Publishers*
25 Ryde Road, Pymble, Sydney NSW 2073, Australia
31 View Road, Glenfield, Auckland 0627, New Zealand
A 53, Sector 57, Noida, UP, India
77–85 Fulham Palace Road, London W6 8JB, United Kingdom
2 Bloor Street East, 20th floor, Toronto, Ontario M4W 1A8, Canada
10 East 53rd Street, New York NY 10022, USA

ISBN: 978 0 7322 9059 7

Cover and internal design by Natalie Winter
Cover images: woman by Emir Ozsahin/ Flickr;
green material by Tay Rees/ Getty Images;
silhouette of building and background by shutterstock.com
Typeset in 11.5/17pt Bembo by Letter Spaced
Printed and bound in Australia by Griffin Press
70gsm Bulky Book Ivory used by HarperCollins*Publishers* is a natural, recyclable
product made from wood grown in sustainable forests. The manufacturing processes
conform to the environmental regulations in the country of origin, New Zealand.

5 4 3 2   10 11 12

For my brothers Peter and Christopher,
and in memory of Lloyd Street State School

What a woman, my friends! If you had seen her
going out, only one eye visible, with a cloak
of Seville satin, a dark dress with long sleeves,
high-heeled shoes, walking with assurance and
a long stride, I do not know which among you
would have been virtuous enough not to follow
her, if not with your legs, at least with your eyes,
during the brief instant in which she crossed the
road.

La Hija de Celestina *(1612)*
by Spanish novelist, Salas Barbadillo

SEVILLE
MAY, 1616

PROLOGUE

The Cyclops' Eye

*In which the painter's apprentice, Diego Velázquez,
climbs the cathedral tower to the highest point of the
former mosque . . .*

Pacheco has decided we will cease our climb here in the minaret. A Renaissance pinnacle rises even higher, but there's not enough room up there for us to walk around freely, so we come to a halt on the thirty-fifth floor. I lean against a wall, my heart pounding. Hanging over my head are two dozen bells of varying sizes. Some of the bells are as big as carriages, the others as small as water urns; some indeed are hanging so low I could almost reach up and touch them if I'd wanted to.

The bells are neither still nor silent. A strong wind agitates the iron vessels and the small ones jostle around like eggs in boiling water. Standing in the shadow of the belfry I soon cool down. I reach inside my jerkin to unfasten my gloves. Seville is a city of thieves and everything of value has to be chained to our clothes. The chain tinkles as I release each glove and put it on. We jingle with the bells, I think, walking out into the midday sun, my hair blowing in my face. Pacheco, my master, is already setting up his brand new refractive telescope on a raised ledge, near the balcony. Now he's bending forward, taking his first look at the encircling city.

I'm struck by the odd sight of my master's eyeglass cleaving to the telescopic lens. And eyeglass to eyeglass they press, like two masks kissing. Surely sparks will fly out as one convex lens rubs against the other. The thought of glass grating against glass makes me shiver.

Pacheco looks around and shouts, 'Diego, come over here!'

So I do. Down below, in an open-air courtyard in Santa Cruz, some merchants are partaking of a sumptuous banquet. Pacheco tells me there are carafes of red wine blooming like tulips down the length of the table. And enough fruit to deck a market stall. The magnification is so strong Pacheco can see purple figs splitting out of their skins. I smile in wonder.

My master raises a hand to hold my attention.

'Bishop Rizi's down there, Diego. Just come out of an apothecary on the Calle de Sierpes. Carrying some sort of brown parcel. What's he up to, eh? He's crossed the square and is heading for the cathedral. Opening the seminary gate. Gracious, he's looking straight up at us. I swear he can see what I'm doing.'

In his excitement Pacheco knocks the *visorio* and loses sight of Rizi. He soon finds something else of interest though.

'A fight,' he tells me conspiratorially. 'Two knights jousting in a field. Arab horses. Glittering mounts. Grey scales patterning the knights' armour. Beautiful, beautiful. Quite a crowd cheering them on. Rabble-rousers. Pickpockets. Oh no, watch your purses!'

Pacheco, chuckling at the misfortune of those in the distant crowd, reaches for the bottle of Guadalcanal wine that I'm holding ready, and pours himself a glassful.

'It's a tool of God, a Holy instrument,' he says with moist lips. 'What if every man had a telescope resting under his arm? Would it not be possible to end all disputes amicably, if one could see the softness of enemy flesh and the anguish of poor souls in the line of battle?'

Now that it is my turn to look, I hesitate, not wanting to appear too eager. I take 'the Cyclops' Eye', as Pacheco has poetically nicknamed it, and I put my eye to the lens. I see bits and pieces around the cathedral, blurry masonry, pipes and shingles. It's hard to focus. Then the fragments sort themselves into perspective. I find street level and a beggar in a floppy hat jumps up at me. I step back in fright. Take another look. Don't panic, Diego. The beggar in the floppy hat doesn't see you observing his joyless existence. He doesn't know you're watching his furtive fingering of coins in a soiled handkerchief. But this worries me too. If I caught him there by chance and thought nothing of it, it would be all right, but if I chose to look down on him mockingly, then it would be sinful.

I decide to search for people I know. On the blue horizon, the spire of our parish church glitters. Dip the lens and the entire façade of the church becomes visible. This is because it fronts onto the square. A yellow haze of wildflowers is growing through the tiles on our neglected mosque portico. Some colours do stand out from afar. In the square I recognise people sitting under the almond trees. If I could lip-read, I would know what my godmother is saying to my aunt. The water seller is there too, in his brown cloak, standing beside a table studded with diamonds. What is sparkling? Rows of glasses basking in the sun.

I'm looking for someone special. A girl I know called Catarina de Loyola. I see her blue cap bobbing along one street after another. But not all these girls in Mary-blue caps could be Catarina, surely. If I really saw her I'd probably be disappointed. The real Catarina could never compete with the one I've built up in my mind. As much as I want to find her, I half-hope I never will. Catarina is there and there and nowhere. What if I saw her in the company of a young man? It might be better not to know some things about the pageantry unfolding in the town below. At this point I stop looking. I'd like to continue, but by myself, privately. I turn to Pacheco who's waiting for an ebullient response from me. I'm a little boy to whom he's given a new toy and I open my mouth to speak, but the only thought that comes into my head is, 'and the apprentice turned to his master and said nothing'. If there's something sneaky about this practice, it's not the Cyclops' Eye that is at fault, I reflect, gently transferring the telescope into Pacheco's waiting clasp, but the way it can be used, for good or evil.

'What we're looking for happens shortly, just before the sixth hour, around noon,' my master is saying, and I remember the real purpose of our climb to the top of the Giralda tower today. We are here to peep inside the convento of the Mercedarians.

'Only one of us will be able to watch,' Pacheco explains. He hasn't let go of the telescope. He will be the one to watch. But my master has surprised me in referring to me as an equal. I'm as tall as he is, to be certain; I'll be sixteen at the end of the month.

Pacheco's having difficulty reading the scroll that contains the Inquisitor Carlos Zamorana's instructions. The wind keeps tossing it about. The Mercedarian convento will be easy for my master to find with the telescope, because it's in the barrio of San Vicente, not far from where we live. The shape of the buildings will be very familiar to him.

'Find the circular tower, master,' I say, having brought the scroll under control, like a sail on a boat. Pacheco's letting me have a look at the map for the first time.

'The entrance is on the first floor gallery, between the chapel and the monks' quarters to the right,' I say, trying to read Zamorana's minuscule handwriting.

'The round tower I have. Two levels if I'm not mistaken,' Pacheco confirms.

But I can direct him no further because just at this moment I have to clutch hold of him, while at the same time shielding my ears. The bell-tower in which we're standing has come to musical life. The cathedral bells are tolling, over and over, in different configurations. The noise is pounding our eardrums and this seems to affect Pacheco adversely, for he shudders and slides down onto his knees.

The bells' belligerence is brief, thankfully, and we quickly regain our footing. After the bells finish tolling I notice a number of sacristans leave the minaret. (I didn't see the bell ringers arrive because we were looking in the opposite direction, away from the belfry.)

Pacheco has turned back to his inspection of the Mercedarian convento. Any later and he would have missed the moment.

'Boys coming out of the round tower now,' he tells me. 'Lots of them in white frocks. Orphans, choirboys, God's flock. Running and playing ball. Some have tennis bats. Why, there is one little boy wearing black! A black sheep. How about that?' Pacheco is amused.

'Boys disappearing down an opening at the side of the gallery. One friar at the tail of the flock, urging the boys on with a stick. Last one down the hole. The landing is quiet again. No-one is out in the open.'

Instructed by the scroll I exhort: 'Wait, master! Keep your eye on the gallery and the exit where the boys have just disappeared. The procession should arrive about now.'

We pause, the wind tugging at our clothes, buffeting the map.

'A couple have arrived on the gallery,' my master enlightens me. 'Father Rastro. And there's a woman with him.' Pacheco hesitates, then continues, 'It looks like Paula Sánchez. Zamorana wasn't lying. It is surely she.'

'Paula Sánchez!' I can't believe she'd be under a cloud of suspicion. My first love, conceived from the purest of ideals.

It was a secret infatuation. Unreciprocated, yet without anguish. Three years have passed yet my affection remains. So was she other than I imagined her to be? Duplicitous and unworthy of my naive adoration?

Paula. Tall, willowy, with the profile of a Roman goddess. She was thoughtful by nature. Brought us pears from her garden and red onions for my table setting. Had I known we were climbing the Giralda to spy on her, I wouldn't have come.

I peruse the scroll. There are no names mentioned apart from Father Rastro's. Just lines, arrows, the hours of the day, the levels of buildings. A mystifying figure, more like a long-stemmed rose, is perhaps meant to be Paula Sánchez.

Pacheco hasn't looked up. His eyeglass is stuck to the lens. 'Here come the rest of the party. The monk. Ah, and the horse. They're making for the round tower, as predicted. Father Rastro has reached the door and is going inside with the woman. The monk is coming after, leading the horse. They've all gone in; I can see no more.'

Pacheco releases the telescope. I fold the scroll neatly back in quarters and hurry to fill master's goblet.

'They go in every day, at about the same time, though not on the Sabbath,' Pacheco says, swirling the wine in his glass. He's weighing something up in his mind.

'So, when do they come out of the building?' I ask impatiently.

Pacheco looks at me in surprise.

'Zamorana thinks they come out by way of another door. The wanton woman has been seen leaving the convento late in the day.'

The wanton woman? Surely my master isn't talking about the Paula we both know and admire. When I began my apprenticeship with him she was his preferred model. A courtesan by profession, but who would blame her for that? One must make a living somehow in our sinful city.

'She may well have a defensible reason to be in the friary,' my master concedes. 'Paula's a *bewitcher*, not a witch.'

An image of Paula afloat on a broomstick, attended by bats and smirking hobgoblins, flickers through my mind. Denunciations of heresy are far more serious than those of prostitution.

'What will Bishop Zamorana do when we confirm there is foundation to the rumours?' I inquire, still anxious on Paula's behalf.

'If he's prepared to make an enemy of Father Rastro,' says master soberly, 'he will send in a spy to take a closer look.'

CHAPTER ONE

Paula and the Ladder-Man

It's years ago, but the memory comes rushing back. I'm sitting beside my mother in a crowded church, pressing up against her familiar body. I'm not listening to the homily because I'm only seven years old and I don't understand what all the words mean. Instead I'm looking at the paintings on the walls, drawn to the myriad flame patterns on the dress of *Eve Spinning* and the spade pushing deep into earth in *Angel Digging*. Angels don't feel pain, I assume, to be able to dig like that, bare foot on the sharp edge of a spade.

The Nativity is my favourite picture: the Magi horses prancing into the stable while their riders focus on a star. Jesus looks like a doll in a bath and then, ever so quickly, he is a grown man with a beard. I imagine tagging after him, watching him do his tricks with love before the big crowds. I believe what I'm encouraged to believe: that he will appear in our village, and that I will meet him and love him, of course, and that he will love me best of all.

I used to have twenty-three memories of Mama; I know because I was always counting them up. When I'm toiling in the convento, as I am this afternoon, I often slip back into the past. I have to kneel on the floorboards with Father Rastro officiating behind me, pressing a damp cloth against the upturned soles of my feet. It feels like a caress, but it's not supposed to be. I do what I'm told, my arms reach out and I grip the base of a wooden Cross passionately, as though my life depends on it.

When natural light fails I get up off my knees and smooth down my skirt. The monk brings my shoes with the rolled-up stockings and garters inside. I slip them on behind the drapes. Collect my manta and bag and prepare to go. (I'll be back again soon.) Father Rastro escorts me through the building and outside into the heat that clings to my skin like a mask. Tonight, at the convento gate, a sacristan is having trouble lighting a lamp. It starts to catch then keeps snuffing out. Perhaps a damp wick is at fault. On the street, I'm met with glistening cobblestones: it must have rained in the afternoon without my hearing it. Father Rastro wanted me to make a confession today. 'I have my own confessor,' I told him, and that's not completely a lie. I'm just a bit out of practice, that's all.

Walking home is ceremonial, doomed and slatternly. I follow an evil star in an opal sky, keeping one eye covered, as if for protection. The generous moon has been sliced in half. On Triana Bridge I mingle with the crossing animals — it's always congested this time of night. The river plays a duet of oar-dips with the slash of my high-heeled shoes. Barges gliding into shore. Little boats swing like hammocks on their moorings. River calming, I call it. I pause a little longer on the bridge. The vapours will start to rise from the depths as darkness draws nigh. If I stood here all night, the vapours would cover me like a caul. Clip-clop. Clip-clop. I turn and join the march of animals to the far end of the bridge where my hoof-trots cease. Remove my tall shoes and stockings again, to climb the steep and slippery incline. At the top of the riverbank, raucous children scampering around naked. Fight the desire to linger. Hurry on, or I'm going to be late. Turn left, turn right, turn left. Have I left time to wash? Sweat pools in my armpits; the soles of my feet are brown. When I open my front door I play a little game with myself. I pretend it's not my home, but someone else's I'm entering. Today I'm listening extra hard as I cross the threshold. I think I hear a woman sobbing, but it's only my indoor fountain blubbering like a person. Quietly past the kitchen so as not to disturb my maid and slave. Why I sneak in here I don't quite know; these girls know what I'm up to. Indeed, Violeta will have invited my gentleman caller inside. I mount the stairs, pause at my bedchamber door. Buckle my shoes back on. Stand and prepare for the sound I detest — the whistling sound his lips will make as they blow upon mine.

Knock. Knock on my own chamber door. Politely, to alert him, in case he's in a compromising position — fondling my underclothing or dozing with his mouth hanging open. Not a sound from inside. A joke of his? Holding out on me? No. I open the door to find the room empty. It's rare Guido Rizi doesn't turn up. My maid knows why. Apparently my benefactor is organising a funeral tonight. Some sour old cardinal has passed away.

Washed, dressed in a chemise and temporarily reprieved, I escape the heat to my rooftop balcony. Ours is a city of rooftop gardens. I sit behind my jungle-screen of potted plants and scan the skyline of Seville. Rooftops join to each other like people join when they sit up close to watch a pantomime. I could walk across the city's rooftops if I wanted. A few leaps and slides would take me to the other side of Triana. I've seen cats follow similar routes across the balconies. I've seen my own ginger cat Maio sunning himself on a balcony down by the river and I know he only made it there by rooftop stalking and stealth. You might think burglars would use our night terraces to get away quickly, but I've not seen a fleeing burglar while musing on the deepening colours of the sky. Besides, there's naught to steal but heavy plants and chairs, and if you did carry away such things the moonlight would find you out. It would.

A dozen pigeons alight from a rooftop terrace a few blocks from me and a man appears beneath the flock (almost as if he's conjured the pigeons from his hat). The man is waving a long pronged object about. I smile, recognising my 'ladder-man' whom I've been watching for some months now. He uses his ladder to climb from roof to roof, zigzagging his way across Triana. At first I thought he must be a roof-tiler or a chimney stacker. I know he isn't a burglar because he stops to talk to people reclining on their balconies. No-one seems to mind when he jumps down in their midst; they welcome him as an acquaintance. Sometimes he does funny things with the ladder. I've seen him stand on it without backing support. He balances on the ladder like a clown balances on stilts. He's an entertainer of sorts or a man at a loose end. He chats to the balcony residents and wanders around attentively. Then he moves to the next terrace. He places the ladder down flat and bridges the space between buildings.

The ladder-man only ever appears in the evenings, when the sky is murky and the horizons tinged blood-orange. I expect that one day his roamings will bring him closer to my own balcony (if he came near me today I would disappear because of my skimpy attire) but just now he seems to be moving further away, and soon I will need a magnifying glass to check his wanderings. (I haven't bought a telescope, though it's quite the fashion to do so in our town.) Part of me doesn't want to look at the ladder-man too closely. I'd prefer the reason for his gad-abouting to stay a mystery.

When I don't see the ladder-man for a few nights, I sip my lemon tea, curl back in my iron chair and wonder what has become of him.

One evening, after a headier sunset than most, in fact after a sunset when the flaming colours burst the horizon's banks and spread out across the sky like spattered paint, the ladder-man popped up on a balcony very close to mine. I heard him before I saw him, because his ladder has a tinkling bell tied to one end that is obviously intended to warn people of his approach. He came so close I could see his narrow hairpin shape and the glow of a youthful cheek. He couldn't see me, hunched behind my potted palms. But I could see him. And then I could see my neighbour

Señora Salamanca. She handed the scrawny intruder a coin for some service rendered, but I'm not sure what the service was.

The ladder-man isn't dressed like an artisan or a clown. He has the look of a shepherd about him, wearing a rustic shift, his ladder a kind of crook with no sheep in sight.

That evening I cowered behind my plants in case the ladder-man came over to me, but he moved off in another direction, as did my hungry eyes after him.

Tonight the ladder-man is swallowed up by the shadows between buildings. I wait to see if he will resurface and when he doesn't I return indoors; follow the wheaten yeasty smell of bread downstairs to the kitchen where my maid and black slave are preparing the evening meal. I join them for some female company; sit at the solid table and preside over their crushing of garlic and herbs. I savour these moments, my feet resting on baked earth — a maid peeling carrots at one elbow, a slave mincing onions at the other. Violeta and Prospera, from near and far.

Tables anchor a person to others, I'm sure. Sitting down and resting one's elbows on a flat surface an order of events is established; an arrangement of hatching smiles and tilting chins. At the centre of the table, fresh eggs nestle in a pure white bowl and near my right hand, chopped vegetables are piled in dewy freshness. I sit to be nourished. My hand reaches out and I crunch on raw carrots until Violeta protests I'm eating tonight's soup.

I would sit here forever, I think, if I could. My grey silk gown is waiting upstairs, Violeta prods. She doesn't need to remind me Bishop Rizi will be here soon. Banished from my own kitchen, I return to my chamber to find the aforesaid gown spread out across my four-poster bed. That's how I'll look when I'm wearing it too! I wonder if my maid was intentionally mocking me laying out my gown in this way, a cushion where my head should be, my slippers (pointing down as if I'm standing on tip-toe) placed as imaginary feet. The scamp has pretended it's a real person lying in wait on the bed. Violeta got the giggles doing this perhaps. My slave, Prospera, would have been more wary of my reproval. It's true, the ten-foot wide skirt does need the breadth of a four-poster to do it justice. It's a mighty bedspread of a dress indeed.

I scoop up the gown and drape it carefully over a chair so it doesn't crease. The task ahead is to turn myself into a woman of quality, which, in our expansive times, is not always distinguishable from a woman of quantity. A puffy skirt will aggrandise my lower realms and hidden wig-pieces will bush the upper kingdom of my hair into playful bounty.

The initial tussle is about to begin: the extraction of my whalebones from the closet. I'm leaning inside, compressing the bones so the ungainly contraption can fit through the doorway. The undergarment bursts free, almost winding me as it springs back into shape with a wailing ping. I catch my breath and clamber up onto the bed, dragging the whalebone wands after me. Lying on my back I undertake to pull the bell-shaped armour on, buttocks and legs raised in the air. Caged, I get up awkwardly, tie the strings at the back and waddle across to my waiting gown. This is the part I love. To embrace the cascade of slippery silk. To raise on high. Offer up to Heaven. (This is why I like to dress on my own, without Violeta or Prospera's help.)

Suspended above my head in a cloud-shaped mass, the gown drops down on me like a curtain, sliding over my face and shoulders. The bliss of robing, so silky and sensual, reminding me of another memory, of my mother hooping me, catching me as if I were a butterfly with my little girl frocks.

I lift the bunches of fabric to cover the circumference of the farthingale. Lace the bodice tightly and now I'm a swan, gliding to the mirror, my undercarriage swaying beneath me. A pile of feathers, ribbons and scarves sits on the dresser. I dip into this maze of tangled softness and pull out my Marie de' Medici ruff. Coil the tripe-like appendage around my neck. Clip at the back and oh ivory froth! The ruff, the ruff, the ruff. How flatteringly it narrows my face and accentuates my cheekbones. I can't help but smile. Frill and foam at the neck, I do. Can such buffoonish excess be allowed? Only the Sevillian nobility still wear them, rather than the high linen collars that are the recent style. But I'm not wearing the ruff to a party tonight. I'm entertaining at home.

Guido Rizi, who's late due to the passing of a sour old cardinal, will probably overcome my defences and succeed in removing all my protective layers. Flirtation and embraces won't be enough to satisfy him. I can already feel his surly hands at the back of my neck, loosening the clasp on the ruff. If I resist, it'll give him more pleasure. What he likes most is to prise my petals open after they've retracted. The more I squeal and avert my face, the more passionate his kisses become. But I can sometimes divert his attention by plying him with spicy condiments and brandied preserves. Then he may fall asleep without exacting his full due.

I stand before the mirror, augmenting my hair, and as I always do when I consider my face at this ruefully expectant time, just before he arrives, I wonder by what calamity of mistaken roads I've come to be here, confronting a visage of just such a person as myself with just such a misplaced expression.

And I confess to you that tending to Bishop Rizi's probing sex that needs to be milked each dawn like a cow's distended teat, is not as bad as watching my mother fall asleep when I was nine and sleep for a week and not ever wake up. It is nowhere near as bad as the drunken-when-I-wasn't-drunk childhood years that followed, when I wandered about in a cloudy haze. The knocking phase I remember clearly: my father locked in the pantry with the cooking woman and my constant knocking on the pantry door to get their attention. They inside, at their foul business, upsetting pots and pans. My knocking and knocking. The cooking woman shouting at me to leave off.

Nothing in my present life is as woeful as watching my father wasting away, coughing blood, then marrying the cook a month before he died. No slights from others sound as cruel as my step-mother telling me I was too fetching and that she wanted to scratch my eyes out for it. And no hardship is as grim as my first year in Seville — 1605 — the year of the drought.

'The padres will put us in the orphanage,' warned my friend Hortense who'd fled the village with me. We were walking down a Sevillian street when the famous dust-storm struck. I shut my eyes, choked on flying soil. Before I knew what had happened someone had pulled me into a tavern for safety. A mature woman offered me a hot meal and a cot for the night. In the darkness, later, a strange man forced himself upon me, forced himself into me. I laughed with embarrassment. Why was he doing this? It was a mistake. He hasn't recognised me for the wrong person. Instead of fighting him off, which I would have done now, I started talking to him like he was a decent human being.

'It's not rape when the man pays,' responded the female procuress, met by my delayed outburst of tears. She handed me enough money to keep me alive for a week. At dawn I ran away, thinking it was Armageddon, the dust still hanging in the air. Nowhere could I find Hortense. I decided to sleep in a graveyard, close enough to the church to keep the fornicators away, but not so close as to be pocketed by the orphanage.

When my money ran out I knocked on more doors, offering to do anything for a cup of clean water. Knocking on doors or pulling chimes still produces anxiety in me now, years later, when I don't have to beg for a thing. But perhaps I'm haunted by my earlier knocking on the pantry door? Whatever the cause, I will call, shout even, before I resort to knocking in the customary way.

I tell you honestly that tending to Bishop Rizi's needs, knowing full well what I'm doing and feeling in charge of my destiny, is nothing to that first year in Seville when I had to face the onslaught of male hands spouting like jutting gargoyles from doors and windows; male snake-arms riding up my skirt and sliding down my bodice wherever I went. From no man was I safe; both young and old accosted me. Whichever way I turned men were laughing lasciviously, moist purple tongues lolling out of mouths, tongues longer than any I'd ever seen sliding out of orifices and chasing me down the street.

There are four gates into Seville, we are told so often, and I have no doubt that my fate would have been different had I entered the golden city, innocent and fourteen, by one of the other three.

A jangle of chimes at the front door. There's just enough time to apply the facial touch-ups: creamy powder for purification (to make me look a little less expressive) and cerise for balancing animation (to make me look a little more aroused).

Something is different tonight though, and my skin stays clean. I find myself climbing back up to my rooftop for a breath of humid evening air. I can hardly fit through the hatch in my whalebones so I have to squeeze myself through, which means that I end up being jettisoned onto the balcony like a stopper coming out of a bottle. A hot tropical gust puts the wind up my skirts and keeps me on my feet. Thunderstorms are on the way; the plants are all achurn in the gale. My farthingale billows from side to side 'whoa, whoa!' like a horse that is shying beneath me, and I have to hold onto the leaves of a potted palm to keep myself from toppling over.

Attaining balance is sweet and I've no intention of going back down to my benefactor, Guido Rizi. He'll have to drag himself up here and chase me round the plants to procure my favours. I wait for the sound I'm dreading, the sound of the hatch opening. The sound flings itself at me and I squat down behind the potted palm and watch a flannel skirt's twisting approach. It's Violeta with her summons: 'The Bishop, Señorita, is waiting in your chamber.' The sight of Violeta pacifies me and I think I'll do as I'm expected to do, but just as I'm approaching the hatch with my maid's arm looped through mine, Rizi's head appears in the hole and he has that hang-dog, part grateful, part enraptured face when he sees me.

I'm repulsed by his expression more than anything else and I shake off Violeta's clasp. There's nowhere for me to flee, except over onto the next balcony. If the ladder-man can do it I can too, and with a jump, a slip, a rent stocking and a deep graze that makes me yell to Jesus for help, I end up stuck in the snick between our two buildings, hanging onto a bit of rusty spouting for support. I'm crying now, for I can feel blood dripping down my shin. Violeta and the Bishop have run to my aid and Rizi is scalding, 'Are you quite mad tonight, my love?' while holding out a hand. I'm thinking if

I take this hand I'll be hearing the springs of my bed bouncing before very long; I'll be a crushed cripple beneath his barrel-like weight, a fat cork jammed into my cleft.

Just as I'm about to grab his hand — because the only alternative is falling — I hear a bell tinkling on the neighbouring balcony and I turn to see a poppy-red handkerchief twirling towards me. The red kerchief is tied to a ladder of fretted slats and this apparatus is lowered so that I can hold onto the bottom portion. And then the man holding the ladder, releasing hidden strength, lifts me up and across the divide so that I roll indecorously onto my neighbour's rock-hard deck. Something snaps beneath my weight. A whalebone, not me.

I rise and look back at those I've left behind, but I do not laugh. There's too much at stake. Left holding onto the small frame of Violeta, Guido Rizi looks as if someone has withdrawn a plate of food he was just about to consume. He lunges forward as if to climb over after us.

My nimble conspirator shoulders his ladder, snatches my arm and we take flight, my whalebones coming to my aid for they waft me along like a dandelion, and before we know it we have flown from balcony to balcony and are out of sight of my 'benefactor' whom from now on, safely in the ladder-man's company, will aptly be called my 'detractor' instead.

Convince me I've done right, won't you. Stop me from turning back.

Make it so that this is not the ending of the tale, but the beginning of my fantastic adventures with my saviour, the ladder-man: the two of us fugitives among birds, belfries and chimneys.

CHAPTER TWO

Further Musing by Diego Velázquez on the Girl in the Blue Cap

Pacheco and I return to the cathedral at break of day, as has been our recent custom. We're close to completing a fresco of Lazarus and his two sisters for the Archbishop of Seville. We're painting it on a wall in the Chapter House. We converse as we labour. I don't mention yesterday's ascent to the top of the Giralda, or what we saw, as Pacheco has told me to speak of it to no-one. By noon we have completed our day's task. My master and I separate in the nave, each of us to renew our faith in the Lord.

When I'm in the cathedral, I like to pray in a side-chapel known as the Sacristía de los Calices. I enter through the antechamber, sit on my usual bench and stare at a bronze altar-plate encrusted with plentiful cherubim. To the right of the altar, a pure white statue of Our Lady presides. She's of simple design, elegant without ornamentation. First I feast upon the altar-plate's carved frenzy — the cherubim's wings are made of hundreds of tiny convex shells — then I turn towards the plain, ungilded Madonna. I like the contrast, the overwrought, then the understated.

In the darkness of the side-chapel today, a nun is hunched in prayer and over to her left a priest adjusts votive candles on a latticed grille. When the priest turns, I quickly bend my head and close my eyes. Prayer comes as easily to me as getting up in the morning and drying Pacheco's brushes, as I've done each day since I joined the Guild of Saint Luke at the age of twelve.

But I don't pray for long. There's movement up in front. The heavy figure of the nun is rising from her prostration. As she shuffles along her pew I notice she has obscured a smaller woman sitting in the front row; a woman with a silk shawl covering her hair. I can tell that the woman is young because of the slender shape of her shoulders. I pretend it's Catarina sitting up in front. She's draped a cloth over her hair because she's in a church. The blue cap must be in her bag, I suppose.

I watch the woman's slight movements, the barely

perceptible shifting of her arms and shoulders as she twists the rosary. It might be nice to paint her from this angle, especially if she turns her head a little. I could capture the wrinkles of her watered silk shawl with wavy lines of white lead tipped with a copper hue.

I slide to the right for a better view. The profile of her face is still concealed, but I can see her hands twisting the beads. They are a girl's hands, unlined, with the slight puffiness of childhood. The light from the window is shining obliquely on the girl and on the marble statue to her right. Our Lady is spun gold by daylight refracted through amber glass. The golden light is shining full force on the statue, but the afternoon rays also encompass the girl's hands so it looks as if her hands belong with the statue. The praying girl appears to be connected to the energy of Our Lady and also to that of the afternoon sun. I wonder if the girl's hands are going to burn, the light is shining on them so intensely.

Still she doesn't shift her head. The longer I watch, the more I'm convinced that it actually *is* Catarina sitting up front. I feel sick with trepidation and yearning. And why should I be graced with Catarina's presence, of all the young women in Seville who might come in here to pray? Why her, now, and in this unlikely place, my favourite side-chapel where so few come? Would I be interested if my feelings were returned? I'm not sure. Yesterday I was searching for her with the telescope, and now my unvoiced prayers have been answered. My heart is racing, yet I almost hate this young woman for turning into the girl I'm obsessed with.

At the leafy crackle of her rising, I lower my eyes. When I look up again she's walking past. It's someone else. The young woman looks nothing like Catarina. Even my master Pacheco's daughter Juana is better looking.

Embarrassed by my delusion, I get up and leave. In the cloister outside I follow a line of king-priests heading for the high-vaulted nave. Me and my mighty friends bow in unison to the crucifix. The king-priests go one way, towards the apse for vespers, and I the other, towards the exit.

Wooden decks fan out on either side of me, smooth slats peopled with pilgrims. Dozens slump low for the taking, dazed by the sublime altarpiece rising above them. I suspect some are merely dozing though. What if you could see a prayer come out of a body? Emerge from a head like soot from a chimney. That would be telling. Nine emissions a day or else! I search for smoky tendrils rising from the proffered heads and detect a few of these incendiary impulses spiralling up to Heaven amidst the purifying veils of Holy incense.

Departing the cathedral grounds I enter the maze-like quarter of Santa Cruz. I'm on my way back to Pacheco's, opening and closing wrought-iron gates as I go. As a child I came in here to get lost and dizzy. Sometimes among friends, we'd hoist each other up to pluck ripe grapes. Today, the snare of narrow streets and the hot sun filtering through the twisting vines merely make me sweat. Exiting the canopied maze, I stop to buy water from a vendor, securing my purse after paying. The water seller, a man of about twenty, pours water from an urn into a pewter tankard. He hands me the tankard very carefully, cupping it underneath so that the precious water won't spill. I consider the water seller. Has he wiped his face and arms with mud to protect them from the sun? This man needs a bath. I try to figure out if the water I'm being offered is clean, but the tankard casts a shadow and I cannot tell. I drink the water anyway, because I'm so thirsty and it would be harder still to refuse. I walk on, perturbed by the taste left in my mouth.

Heading west I'm overcome by the aroma of the soap factory in San Salvador. The soap being manufactured gives off a pungent fragrance of ripe olives and cleanliness. The smell reminds me of Catarina, because I first saw her round the corner from here, in San Salvador square. The Loyola sisters were dancing a chaconne that day. It was carnival; the four of them were wearing gold eye-masks and I could barely tell them apart. The sisters were calling Catarina's name, and I found myself looking around for this 'Catarina', whom I imagined was the centre of things. After the dance, the four sisters arranged themselves in a small circle and I heard her name again. So that was her! The girl wearing the blue cap. I could see neither her expression nor her hair, but something else captured my attention. Catarina's skirt was very dusty, giving the impression that she was connected to the ground in some way. She had probably sat on flagstones to watch the pageant, or walked along an unmade road earlier in the day. Perhaps it was a carnival game that was at fault. The condition of her attire intrigued me because I often went home with paint and grime on my clothing. We had something in common.

I moved up close so I could hear what she was saying to her sisters. Catarina's voice was melodious yet urgent; a compelling combination. The plan she was unfurling had to do with winning the big carnival prize of a pack-saddle. It was not the Loyola family dog that was going to attempt the jump and win the saddle — their own dog was too short to hurdle the bough — but the hound of an ale-drinking friar.

As I watched, the Loyola girls managed to seek out the most athletic dog at the carnival and convince the dog's owner to relinquish his animal and his own good prospect of winning the prize. Perhaps the owner was too drunk to notice or care; perhaps he never indulged in carnival games. All I can tell you is that I saw the friar give up his dog magnanimously to the girls a short time later. I observed the dog-jumping spectacle with amusement, and I was also nearby when the champion beast was returned to the friar along with a jar of preserves. My final memory was of the four triumphant sisters lugging the saddle home, almost tripping each other up as they cradled its cumbersome weight.

Catarina makes things ripen into a story, I'm thinking, as I pass through the square today. And she's an eldest child too, by the looks of her. Just like me.

Nearing San Vicente, my home barrio, I find myself walking along the high southern wall of the Mercedarian convento. Broken glass shines formidably along the top row of bricks. On the other side is a convento orchard. Youthful chatter in the trees wafts over the wall. Children are involved in a gardening enterprise. I stand back from the road and strain my neck to get a better look. A child in a white cassock is perched high up a tree. He's picking apricots which he passes down to an outstretched hand. I can only see the arm of the lower boy. Early for apricots, I think, but this tree is one of those African varieties that has two summer flowerings.

I return to the road and keep walking. If my master's prediction is correct, the Inquisitor Zamorana is about to send a spy inside these walls. I taste the unclean water in my mouth again. Will the convento superior, Father Rastro, and the courtesan, Paula Sánchez, sense themselves being watched and feel mistrusted? Will they even do something to implicate themselves?

I might pay a visit to the Mercedarian convento tomorrow. I have a good enough reason to do so. A young boy I sketched last year is living among the friars. (His confinement in the convento is something I've blamed myself for.) When I started drawing the boy, Luis, I didn't realise that he was a Morisco. One of Pacheco's friends was looking at my drawing and he recognised Luis as one of them. Shortly after this happened, Luis and his family were detained by the authorities. His mother and sister were deported.

As I get closer to Pacheco's, my first contact with Luis comes floating back, like a huge soap bubble preserved from the suds of the past.

'I want you to sit for me.'

Luis, who looks about eleven, seats himself in front of me. I'd been watching him peddling oranges in the laneway outside my master's house.

'I mean I would like to draw you,' I explain.

Luis stares uncomprehendingly at me.

'I want you to pose laughing, and hold that pose. Can you do that?'

'I'm not for sale,' Luis says, standing up defensively.

'What? Oh, no. Not for sale,' I agree.

Luis is still looking at the door, but eventually he does as I ask. He tries to laugh naturally. He manages to hold a laugh stiffly on his face.

I make the drawing and put it aside.

'I want you to cry this time. Can you do that?'

'I never cry. Only when I burnt my arm.'

Luis draws my attention to a bubbly purple scar that runs the length of his forearm.

'That's a nasty scar,' I say in sympathy. Then I reach over and pick an onion from the midst of my kitchen tableau, and set about slicing the dark skin from the surface with a blade. I hand the onion to Luis who guesses what I mean him to do with it. He holds the peeled bulb up to his eyes. He's crying now, and I'm drawing faster than normal, the red pencil dancing in my hands.

Luis is mean, happy and dreamy in succession.

'This is a solemn face, Luis. Drop your jaw. Copy me!' I make faces at Luis and Luis makes faces back. This part he seems to enjoy.

At the end of two weeks he asks if he can take the drawings away with him. I explain that they belong to my master. I tell Luis not to worry, because Pacheco has promised the drawings won't be sold.

'Mama says it's bad luck to leave mirrors of yourself behind,' Luis complains. He reaches for the money that I've left on the table for him, picks up his hat and satchel full of oranges and walks towards the door. Then he turns around and pokes out his tongue before rushing from the room.

CHAPTER THREE

Paula Learns the Tricks of the Ladder Trade

The first step to freedom, they say, is imagining it — I'm spending more time with the ladder-man these days. I've found that he is a kind of balcony prince, welcome on many rooftops where owners greet him as a relative or friend. Some Triana residents have even made low tin shelters for him to sleep under. Why is he so loved and accepted? People give him a coin in exchange for nothing more than a beautiful smile or a gracious bow. But then I catch him at his business. Watering the balcony plants for neighbours who are out of town or too busy to do it themselves. He also provides water and seeds for caged birds. And enjoys doing it — his little secret.

The ladder-man's first task, after he's bandaged my knee with the red kerchief, is to teach me to balance on his ladder. Why I need to learn this trick is not quite clear. However, I'm prepared to try the stunt to make him happy. The ladder-man holds the ladder up while I climb the lower rungs. Then he says, 'Ready?', and I nod. He lets go of the ladder but of course I can't hold my weight. I jump off quickly. I'm not going to get the hang of it. Balancing on a ladder is not going to be my strength, like it is his. But we try, again and again.

'I'm just learning to tip over doing this,' I complain. He takes a piece of charcoal from his pocket and writes on the cement at our feet: 'To fall is to balance.'

The ladder-man writes everything down because he doesn't speak. Rather than making me fearful of him, this impediment has the opposite effect. A mute man is not really a man to be scared of at all. Besides he has a gentle narrow face and soulful eyes. I've learnt to trust a man by his eyes; there's nothing predatory about the way the ladder-man looks at me. And he has graceful hand movements to back up his graceful smile. He pulls out a charcoal or chalk whenever necessary. Now he writes a few questions on the wall of the building.

— Name?

'Paula,' I say aloud, then wonder if I should have given him a false name, like Zonda or Amira.

— Married?

I shake my head, but then think I should have said I was, for a bit of extra protection.

— Hungry?

At this I hesitate, because I am just at that mid-point where you are happy either to eat or do without. Finding me undecided he takes a nutcracker and some almonds from his pocket and breaks them open. The shells he collects and puts back in his pocket. He's very neat and tidy like that. He doesn't seem to have any obvious faults, though I can't help commenting on his hairpin shape.

'You're very thin.' It's a rude thing to say but it wasn't meant as a put-down. His meagre frame is the most obvious thing about him.

He nods and writes on the wall. 'Always thin.' He wants me to know he isn't fasting or ill.

The ladder-man then writes a sentence that I can't understand because I don't know all the words. I blush and pretend to understand. Oh dear, he must have been able to see through my pretence. He must have worked out I can't read properly because he never writes a long sentence for me again. But I'm not a total ignoramus. Little words I know, as do most unschooled people.

To fall is to balance. I ponder this paradox. Maybe the combination of these words means something else in written language. Or maybe what the ladder-man really means is that to fall is to desire balance all the more. Certainly each time I fail to keep the ladder upright, I'm furious with myself. I try even harder next time. Indeed I'm getting muscles in my legs from so much practice. I've learnt to avoid smackbang falls and eggplant bruises.

But maybe the ladder-man really does mean to fall is to balance. Exactly that. In falling I'm giving gravity its due. Succumbing to nature's laws. *He*, in balancing on a ladder, is defying gravity, is upsetting balance. Oh, come on Paula. Just who are you trying to bluff?

'Will I ever learn to do it?' I ask after a few seconds of magical equilibrium have been followed by another topple. He smiles and writes 'of course' in charcoal across the cement. Well at least he has faith in me.

I never stay with the ladder-man too long after dusk. It's difficult communicating with someone who keeps his mouth shut all the time. Because he reveals so little about himself, I end up revealing *more* about myself. His muteness is having the effect of turning me into a chatterbox. Hmm, I am not sure that I like this new me; I was more guarded in the past. Having to talk all the time is exhausting. And there's another reason I like to get away from him sooner rather than later: I don't want the ladder-man to think I *need* his company. This might make him feel he has some obligation to me and then he might not want to see me any more.

I do wonder why this young man lives as a rooftop shepherd when he can read and write and could earn much more money as a scribe. His muteness wouldn't worry the clergy. They would see it as a strength — this man has truly taken a vow of silence — or else they'd take pity on him. Either way they would welcome him into their midst. Yes, the ladder-man would be better off finding gentlemanly work of some kind.

The next time we meet I take the ladder-man's charcoal and write three questions challengingly across the flaky cement:

— Name?

— Married?

— Hungry?

He considers me with a wistful expression on his face, takes the charcoal from me and draws a neat cross after each question. I accept he's neither married nor hungry, but why doesn't he want me to know his name? Everyone has a name, don't they? Well, no point forcing the issue. I borrow his nutcracker, crack open some walnuts and go on a feeding frenzy.

I've got into the habit of helping the ladder-man with his balcony chores. He waters the plants and sweeps the decks while I seed the birdboxes and feed the animals. We have one assignment for every fifth house, on average. The rest of the people give us 'right of passage' across their balconies and galleries; we are dependent on their generosity and accordingly very grateful. Some make the ladder-man pay a tithe to cross. Others close their eyes and wave us past, as though they want us off their premises quickly. Most are welcoming, even if they don't employ the ladder-man in any capacity. If the residents are sitting outside admiring the sunset they might converse with us briefly. Out of kindness, some give the ladder-man a few coppers because they know he doesn't have much more than the rustic shift he always wears. That rustic shift has seen better days. I've sewn him a new gown because I can't stand the foul reek of the old one. I've decided to sew him one gown a week because they're so easy to make, just loose hessian sacks really, with a girdle for the waist that I don't have to sew. It might be offensive to ask if I could launder his smelly shift.

Tonight, as we are performing yet another balcony watering assignment, I take time out to ingratiate myself with a Trianese couple who are sitting on their rooftop 'balcony bird-watching' as we call it. I'm in a prying mood, and out of the ladder-man's hearing, I ask the couple if they know what the ladder-man's Christian name is. But they say he's just called the ladder-man. They don't know his actual name. Doesn't he have a real name, I persist? Of course he would have one, they reply. 'We just don't know it, that's all. Can't you see he's mute? You can't expect him to go around introducing himself to all and sundry,' they tell me. And ladder-men have to be very discreet to keep their jobs, they add.

I'm onto this one really quickly. Are there *other* ladder-men? I ask.

Sure, they say. For each barrio there are several ladder-men. Sometimes many. Sometimes too many. Pointing towards the horizon where the moon is sitting huge and wet (like it's just taken a dip in the ocean) I follow my neighbour's finger and see a tiny ant-sized man poised on a terracotta roof. And there's a pointy object jutting out from him that must be his ladder. 'There's another ladder-man right there!' the neighbours say. They laugh when they see my thwarted expression. 'There are dozens,' they claim. 'Simply dozens.'

I'm crestfallen because I thought mine was the only ladder-man in existence. My neighbour offers me his brand new telescope to have a better look at the crop of ladder-men stretching across the skyline of Seville, but I close my eyes and shake my head. I don't want to see reality when fantasy suits me better.

'You're not the only ladder-man in Seville,' I say to him when we're taking shelter from a storm later that evening.

Saying this I feel as if I'm throwing a stone in a still pond and waiting for a momentous reaction. Not a muscle moves in the ladder-man's face. (Of course my news is no news to him.) I'm relieved to see he's not hurt by my accusation. Women know there's trouble brewing when they meet an injured look. Men's hurt is different from women's hurt. Even I know that. Women may be pathetic in comparison to men when it comes to bearing cuts and bruises, but women are stronger when it comes to emotional affronts. Even I know that.

The next time we pass by these neighbours' lands, the ones with the telescope, I sidle deferentially up to them and do a bit of further fishing.

'Does the ladder-man have a wife?' I pry.

The neighbours titter. Their faces say, what is this lass going to ask us next?

'Not that we know of,' they reply, shaking their heads. 'But there is a ladder-*woman*.'

'A ladder-woman,' I say in fright, imagining a shepherdess with muscular legs who has mastered the art of perfect balance. I picture a woman who can balance a basket on her head at the same time as hang off a ladder without a wall to lean against. A ladder-woman would be a greater rival than a wife because she would be up here on the roofs doing what I am trying to do but doing it better than I.

They do not leave me in agony much longer.

'It is *you*,' they say, with much amusement.

'Oh,' I respond, and fake a laugh.

I wish I could think of something witty to say in return. But the ladder-man would be upset if I offended this gracious couple. The only time he has really chastised me was when I addressed a female neighbour with a beard as *señor* by mistake.

'Your blabber mouth will cost me a job,' the ladder-man wrote in chalk on a slate he keeps in his shelter for serious conversations. The ladder-man made sure I knew exactly what his words meant because he made me read them aloud two or three times as he held my wrist so tight I couldn't get away.

'How was I supposed to know she was a woman? She doesn't look anything like one.'

I got a bit wary of him after that and didn't go back for a while because I wasn't sure he was as gentle as he'd appeared to be.

But before long Bishop Rizi was back in my bed slipping jewellery under my pillow and the only way I can cope with the sense of panic and revulsion that rises up in me when this happens nowadays, is to spring up onto my balcony and call out for my ladder-man. Usually he'll hear me if he's not too far away, he'll come a clack-clacking with his nutcracker, his pockets bulging with walnuts and almonds and we'll go off on a jaunt together.

One night when the ladder-man and I were sweeping the landing of a deserted gallery (the grandée owners of this big house are always away in Granada or Málaga), he did indeed christen me his 'ladder-woman'. He wrote down that he had a surprise for me, something that I would find very useful. He drew me behind the shelter and pulled from under some rags a second ladder, one with both a copper bell the size of a tulip and a white kerchief, tied to the top rung.

I know I should have been pleased with this gift from the ladder-man. It was a sign of his acceptance of me, his assistant. If I'd wanted to, I could also have seen it as a token of his affection. Instead, when he handed me the ladder, I jumped to the conclusion that I was being rejected. He didn't want to share his ladder with me any more. He wanted me to fork out on my own, become more self-reliant. That was the meaning of the gift.

I pretended to be pleased though. My mother was with me long enough to teach me basic manners. I knew he would want me to test the ladder out, so I stood it against the side wall of the gallery, next to the shelter where the ladder-man resides from time to time, and I climbed up to the top rung and plucked the bell into life. Clang! Clang! The rungs feel strong, I decide, coming down again. Shrewdly I'm thinking that even if I haven't learnt to balance on a ladder without support, I can put this one to good use climbing from one balcony to the next. I won't have to borrow the ladder-man's equipment all the time and we can work on separate balconies if we need to. In fact, when things get unbearable with Bishop Rizi, I can bridge my own balcony and not have to rely on the ladder-man to lift me over. Of course it is a loving gift!

It's midnight and time to return to my post beside Guido Rizi who was last heard (but not seen) puffing in his sleep. But instead I agree to stay with the ladder-man further into the night. He takes my ladder and places it alongside his own that's resting against the shelter. Comparing mine to the ladder-man's in the fuzzy halo of the lantern's light, I notice that it looks a little more squat and female than his does. The wood on mine has been sand-papered smooth and stained a lovely treacle colour, whereas the other ladder's rough and grey. Yes, mine is a female ladder. No chance of splinters or calloused fingers from handling the rungs.

I stand there admiring the pair of ladders. He does too. We are both doting fools. The ladder-man points to the sky; it is folding in on itself like a house of cards collapsing in a flailing wind. There is nowhere else to go but inside, under the shelter.

When I enter the ladder-man's cramped lair and kneel down, my skirt (minus the farthingale which I never wear up here on top deck) spreads out around me and I feel as if I'm sitting in the middle of a big puddle. The ladder-man must think we're in an Arabic bath with this amount of silk swamping everything around. He smiles, keeping his lips pressed closed (he always keeps them closed when he smiles) and picks up the regal tide of my skirt and carries it around with him while he readies himself to sleep. He's a skinny dragon with a wrap-around tail. He lies down next to me and I look into his river-brown eyes that make resting beside him so easy. He grips my skirt tight. I slip my hand in his pocket, take out a knob of chalk and hold it out to him.

'Please tell me your name.'

I can't go forward without his name. But he looks away and I can see he won't comply, so I speculate that he must have done something bad down there when he lived among streets and horses. He doesn't want me to know his name because his reputation is smeared, like mine is.

'Did you commit a felony down there?' I ask all agog, and he looks at me in distress; then I find his body and face retracting before my eyes and I realise I'm losing my attachment to his aerial world. The scene changes abruptly as in a dream and I'm back in my bedchamber lying beside

Guido Rizi who is still puffing in his sleep like a man who's short of breath. Rizi is sweating. He smells like the venison stew we ate this evening. Violeta's specialty. I tell myself to 'get up Paula'. Search in the dark for the perfume shaker. Douse sheets and furniture; drive the dribble-scents away.

I'm wishing I hadn't accused the ladder-man of wrongdoing. Would someone of such doe-eyed sweetness be capable of wickedness?

I fall asleep with the toneless words of the ladder-man grunting recrimination in my ear: 'If you don't trust me you don't deserve me,' (his voice scraping like a keel on the riverbank, his voice, alas, with no defining timbre to it at all) and I'm so cross with myself that when I finally fall asleep I dream of cutting out my slack fool's tongue with the thread of my sewing yarn.

CHAPTER FOUR

In the Mercedarian Convento with Diego Velázquez

After I complete my early morning work for Pacheco, I pack some sweets and nuts in a bag and go to call on the Mercedarians. I ring a bell at the front gate and wait, assuming that the apprentice of the devout Pacheco will be welcomed with immediate trust. An orderly arrives, asks me my business, then admits me to the vestibule where paintings of previous Mercedarian leaders line the walls. I pretend to admire these ghastly pictures while the orderly goes to find Luis.

It's more than a year since I've seen him and he's much taller and even a little plump. Gone are his street clothes and bare urchin feet. He's wearing a white cassock and brown leather sandals. When I give him the sweets and nuts, he smiles broadly and asks me, very directly, if I'm here to make some more drawings of him. His attitude is less recalcitrant than in the past; it's almost as if he wouldn't mind sitting for me.

'You're happy in here?'

Luis thinks about it, then shakes his head. 'They force us to eat pork. They even make us drink wine. We must sing Gregorian chants three times a day!'

Luis was allowed to stay in Spain because of his lovely singing voice.

'How many Morisco boys are in here with you?' I inquire.

'Um. There's Benito, Remi and Camilo.'

'The others, have they been here long?'

Luis nods. 'They were really little when they came.'

'How do you find school?'

'Okay, I guess.'

Luis looks at me glumly. 'I've heard nothing about my mother and sister,' he pauses and, when I don't comment, he continues, 'Where would they have settled do you think? They say our people are welcome in Tunis, but meet death elsewhere. In Algiers and Morocco they call us Christian infidel. Remi's father was murdered by bandits on the road to Fez. And you know what? The priests waited three years to tell him.'

41

'I've heard similar stories,' I say.

'Can you help us escape?'

I'm taken aback by his naive trust. 'Do you really wish to join your mother in the Mohammedan lands?'

My question has puzzled him.

'None of us *really* wants to go to the Barbary States,' Luis continues, 'We're Sevillians, aren't we? We've been baptised in the name of the Holy Ghost, just like you. We want to go back to eating couscous in our old homes, but that isn't possible, is it?'

I shake my head.

As an eleven-year-old I looked on while thousands of Moors were driven from our city, weighed down by their heavy bags. The river of people was passing by for ages it seemed, and when it ceased I remember seeing lots of baggage left lying on the road. The Moors couldn't carry all their belongings with the crowds moving so fast, so they dropped it as they went. A day later and all the forsaken bags and furniture had been scavenged. But the exiled Moors left curses on their abodes in West San Marcos and Adarjevo. Walls collapsed on unsuspecting new residents, and one poor family ate from a garden of poisoned vegetables and three of them died. The barrios where the Moors lived have become ghost towns since then. Horses refuse to take their riders into these suburbs, but children play round the fringes, trespassing inside for thrills and dares.

Luis and I need a change of scene. At my request a priest is happy to guide us around the chapter house. Paintings by my master Pacheco are prominently displayed and appear to be in excellent condition. As soon as the priest leaves, Luis relaxes. He sits down, his back resting against a wall, and plays absentmindedly with the buckles and straps on his sandals. I continue my inspection of the paintings and pretend to take notes, but the main reason for my visit never leaves my mind. I make sure we slip outside onto the first floor gallery and are in the vicinity of the round tower just before noon when the choirboys are due to be released from morning school. While Luis tries to peer in the windows of the tower at his friends, I call him back. Trying to sound casual, I ask him a number of questions about the circular building, but Luis seems to have lost interest in conversing with me.

It is our schoolhouse, he replies with effort. Yes, it was going to be a watchtower, and taller than the gold tower on the river, but the money ran out because the new chapel cost so much, he explains begrudgingly. But the tower's still growing, he adds with a twinge of irony. It hasn't reached its full height yet, he assures me with a sly look. I assume he's pulling my leg so my inquiries cease.

The sun is directly overhead and I know that the bells will ring at any moment. In the distance I can see the top portion of the Giralda rising above the other Sevillian buildings but I'm too far away to tell if there are faces looking down from the minaret where Pacheco and I were standing two days ago. What if my master has gone up there with his new telescope and I'm found out? Would he value my daring, or punish me for it?

I notice we're not alone on the first-floor gallery. Down the other end is an artisan whitewashing walls. He keeps looking around at me and this makes me nervous. If he turns out to be Zamorana's spy what an odd situation, for then I would be spying on the spy. And the spy would be spying on me. I tell myself that I've broken no law as yet. There's no need to worry about being here under false pretences.

The bells chime the sixth hour of prayer and shortly afterwards a door is flung open and schoolboys come volleying out. They catch hold of Luis as they gambol past. Some of these choristers try to take Luis with them, but he resists, fending off their clutching hands, smiling charmingly as he does. Luis is in my care and he doesn't have to join the others. And to be singled out seems to please him.

The boys' chattering fades as they disappear down the stairs at the end of the landing. Shortly afterwards the adult pageantry that I've been waiting for begins and my heart starts beating faster. Coming onto the landing is Father Rastro accompanied by Paula Sánchez. Behind them, the monk leading the horse. All is unfolding as Pacheco bespoke it in the Giralda. When I see these larger-than-life figures heading towards me I want to run and hide behind the round tower. But it's too late to do anything conspicuous, so I stay where I am. The procession comes to a halt. Paula has recognised me and a tremor runs down my spine. At the sight of Paula's red dress, I'm transported back two years in time.

I don't know Paula very well, but I do know her red dress. I was thirteen when I found that very dress (or an earlier version of it) hanging in Pacheco's studio. She'd been modelling for my master and had left it behind. Late at night I removed the dress from its hanger and made my first entry into the Garden of Eden. I recall as though it were yesterday, the feel of Paula's velvet skin, smooth against my own, the rub and weave of it, the dress alone, and how close the fabric came to tearing as I stretched it across my reclining body. My fear of tearing the fabric won out over the temptation to tear it, to puncture her velvety contours. I learnt the shape of Paula's body from the shape of her dress as I wrapped the cloth, her bodily shape, around my own skinny torso. My erotic pulse was awakening; I fought with the dress as though it were a wild animal. And now, staring at Paula in her familiar tactile costume, I'm looking at the skin of a wild animal that has come back to haunt me. The animal has been skinned and sewn up for a woman to wear. Paula's dress reminds me of stealth, of taking the dress from the hanger in Pacheco's studio and of my thirteen-year-old terror of being caught out. Today, the sight of red swirls, the cut and tuck of embroidered sleeves and the curve of the gown below Paula's neck brings back the smell of her under-arm sweat and a familiar odour of musk, vanilla and rising yeast that wasn't just Paula's, but my own mother's, retained from an earlier childish intimacy. At night, in secret, I wore and wore Paula's dress. I crushed it between my thighs and frayed it thin. Then each morning, at dawn, I hung it up in Pacheco's studio for Paula to wear when she next came to sit for him.

And, as far as I know, I've never been found out.

Paula is beckoning me over. I wave self-consciously and walk towards the party suspected of infamy. Luis lags behind me. Paula introduces Father Rastro who's holding a crown-of-thorns in the crook of his arm. On closer inspection I can see it's a bird's nest. Full of featherless chicks. It's an odd thing for him to be carrying, for sure.

'Pacheco's apprentice? How much time do you have?'

Father Rastro invites me into the round tower. He directs Luis back to where the boys in white frocks have gone. Luis waves at me with a resigned expression. I tell him in parting I will come and say goodbye before I leave. He seems satisfied with this and off he bounds.

I'm about to enter the suspect building with the equestrian party, but just before I go inside, I glance around the gallery and I can't help noticing a look of envy on the face of the artisan whitewashing the walls. How that man would love to be wearing my shoes. Inquisitor Zamorana is a fool, I think, and his spy is wasting his time, for if a young man of excellent reputation, such as myself, is being invited into the round tower, whatever's going on inside can hardly be heretical or even terribly sinful.

We're standing in a schoolroom among numerous desks and slates. The close smell of children's bodies lingers in the air. The monk makes for a stairwell on the left. He guides the horse up the stairs. The animal follows obediently, but it's a slow, awkward ascent. Then Rastro, with his prickly nest, and Paula and I follow.

The windows on the upper level are covered with drapes and the room is dark. Paula crosses the floor to tie back a curtain and open a window. Incoming light reveals hay in the corner and a trough of water for the horse. I breathe in a penetrating odour of vinegar and linseed oil, receiving my first clue as to what's going on up here. Everything makes sense when I see the huge stretched canvas looming on the other side of the room.

A large painting of a penitent Magdalen presides. It looks very close to completion. There are two persons in the foreground of the painting and, to their right, the horse. Paula is kneeling before a Cross and the figure kneeling behind her is Father Rastro. He's wiping her feet with a pearl-coloured cloth. The Mercedarian leader is kneeling side-on, as is Paula, though she has more of her back to the viewer. You only can see the right side of her face. A mussel-blue veil is draped over her hair, the artist giving an underwater look to the dark undulations of the fabric. Paula clings to the barren Crucifix, her velvet dress gathered up around her knees, exposing her bare calves. I'm thinking the calves of a woman shouldn't be revealed before a Cross. Nor should a penitent be giving her redeemer a seductive eye. This will make my master Pacheco fret, it will.

The young monk accompanying us is also in the painting. He's standing in the recesses, behind the horse. For confirmation that the two monks match, I look at the *real* monk who is lifting the *real* Cross from the floor and resting it up against the imitation altar. This young man looks Arabic. He's possibly a fully-Christianised Moor. After eight centuries of interbreeding, there's no shortage of Arab blood swimming in Andalusían veins. I too might be partly Moor, I reflect, then dismiss this as improbable given what I know of my ancestors. The monk is returning my stare, so I avert my eyes, looking at the painting again.

The *painted* monk's head and shoulders are rising above the horse's shaggy mane. The monk is holding the bridle casually, in anticipation of a movement forward in time. Or has he just arrived at the altar with the horse? A painting is not just about the immediate moment, Pacheco likes to say; it refers to what has *just* happened and to what is about to happen in the next scene. Guess what will happen next, Pacheco loves to ask his apprentices.

It looks as if the horse is waiting to carry the Magdalen figure away, after the stain has been sanctimoniously removed from her soul. That's the answer I'd give Pacheco if my master were standing beside me now.

My eye is captivated by the *real* Paula who has taken off her shoes, and is in the process of removing her stockings. She does this discreetly, keeping her legs concealed. While I'm watching her, the monk decides to lead the horse to the water. He stops to adjust the rope halter, blocking my vision.

I look at the painting again. Does the artist intend putting a fourth figure to the left of the kneeling Rastro?

There is a discolouration in this place, assuming vaguely human contours. A shadow looms — perhaps the beginnings of a soon-to-be-painted figure. The left side of the canvas could well do with another person to balance the bulk of horseflesh on the right. Indeed the magnified horse's rump takes up nearly a quarter of the canvas, an unseemly intrusion in a healing ritual administered by a figure who is apparently the most worthy forgiver of sins. Father Rastro playing Christ at the Magdalen's heels could well be sacrilegious. It's permissible for the biblical Saints, such as Saint Matthew and Paul, to look like the models playing them, but there should be no variation on images of Jesus. So says the Council of Trent.

Father Rastro breaks my trance, 'Do you approve, Diego Velázquez?'

'Er . . . yes,' I mutter, then pause before adding, 'But I'm not sure everyone will.' Who's the buyer, I'm wondering. It's unlikely Father Rastro would have commissioned this work. It's not in the orthodox Mercedarian style.

'It's enviable, but uhm . . . I'm surprised Father, that you . . . ' I'd like to know why he's sitting for the painting, but I can't afford to be presumptuous.

'Why I have sanctioned this painting and assumed the role of anointer?'

'With a penitent Magdalen?' I inquire.

'With a penitent *woman*,' he corrects me. 'But we are certainly indebted to the tradition of the biblical sinner.'

'And the artist?'

'A gentleman from Antwerp, Harmen Weddesteeg,' Rastro replies.

I've never heard of a painter called by this name. I probably should know who he is, so I nod and change the topic.

'What will become of the dark impression to the left of the altar?' I ask, pointing to the shadow.

'It's the artist's signatory mark,' Rastro explains.

'An impression of himself?' I inquire with much interest.

'A woman he loved, supposedly.'

'A dead woman? A ghost?' I pester.

'He calls it a human cavity. It appears in all his paintings when they're nearing completion. But you can ask him yourself. He'll be down presently,' Father Rastro gestures towards an open manhole in the corner of the ceiling that leads up to the attic. 'Weddesteeg's residing upstairs,' he informs me.

A short time later the pleasing face of a man does indeed appear above our heads like a moon sliding out from between a gap in the clouds. The man waves at us in a friendly fashion. One Harmen Weddesteeg from Antwerp presumably, who swivels himself around onto a stepladder, and makes a spirited descent.

Arriving in our midst, Weddesteeg immediately begins some outrageous flirting with Paula Sánchez. (One-sided flirting, mind you.) Father Rastro seems tolerant of the painter's familiarity with Paula. I notice that the model herself doesn't seem to mind.

The monk hurries forward to give Weddesteeg his palette and brushes. The painter acknowledges me for the first time and Father Rastro makes a belated introduction. Weddesteeg nods acceptingly when I tell him how remarkable I find his penitent woman. 'You're a painter too? Oh, in that case . . . ' And he takes a much greater interest in my compliments.

The figures are taking up their positions for the dramatic narrative — Rastro lifts the cloth to Paula's soiled feet, Paula inclines her face, and the painting begins without delay. They're keeping to a regular schedule it seems.

I stand behind Weddesteeg, feeling a bit out of place. I haven't had a chance to ask him about the human cavity and, more importantly, a question of technical interest, about how he's made the light shine so radiantly on the three figures, and on the horse with its majestic, springy tail.

The shrieking chicks are proving tiresome. What possessed Father Rastro to bring the nest up here? Perhaps Weddesteeg wants them in his painting. Good humouredly, I tell Weddesteeg about my goldfinch, and how I like to paint to its musical accompaniment. When I forget to take the cage to work, I don't paint so well.

Weddesteeg listens respectfully then blurts out: 'Oh, drown the pathetic things and be done with it!'

Rastro, a little flustered, gets up from his genuflection. Retrieves the nest from the table and brings it over to me, holding it out like it's the Eucharist. I open my mouth to protest, but I needn't have worried.

'Diego Velázquez, you can help us out. Find Luis de Pareja. He'll be in the refectory. Get the resident boys digging up worms. Tell them to shake a water can over the birds' beaks.'

This suits me, as I'd intended spending more time with the Morisco boy. Departing the round tower with the nest under my wing, I head down to the refectory. Luis looks surprised to see me carrying the nest. He introduces me to his friends, Benito, Remi and Camilo. These three Moriscos are a good deal shorter and younger than Luis, and they appear to look up to him. Well Remi and Benito obviously do. Camilo seems to exist in a world of his own. He's reading a book as he comes out of the refectory, and he continues to read as we go about our business, holding the words up close to his eyes, as elderly scholars do. A priest has given the boys over into my care and we head for the courtyard to search for grubs in the flowerbeds. After we've fed and watered the chicks as best we can, we lie on the grass beneath some foliage and look up at the sky for a while, (this will pass for siesta, the boys tell me). Little Remi falls asleep in the heat and I cover his face with my handkerchief to protect it from the sun. While we're waiting for him to wake, Benito, Luis and I play knucklebones with the backbones of small animals in a shady cloister. I used to love playing this game with my younger brothers. I forget about the bells, I forget about the painting in the round tower, I forget I ever had another reason for being in the convento than visiting Luis. Camilo continues to read Virgil but he's listening to us with one ear. I know, because he smiles weakly when we laugh. An amazing little chap, Camilo. Later on we discuss *The Aeneid* together as I might do with boys my own age in Latin school.

Luis has come up with what I think is a good idea and, when Remi wakes, the five of us head off in the direction of the orchard. (The boys are supposed to be fruit picking this afternoon.) I carry the nest and Luis and his friends carry two tin pails each. Camilo continues to read as we traipse through the vegetable gardens, surrounded by a flock of white butterflies. Long-legged Luis clambers up an apricot tree with the nest in his arms, securing it beside another nest he's been keeping an eye on. He's hoping against wisdom that the mother will attend to two broods at once. But the hatchlings aren't even the same breed!

I tell Luis to climb down from the tree quickly, and not to disturb the workings of nature. The boys all seem to think Luis's matchmaking will work out well for the swallow chicks.

When Luis says I may eat as much fruit as I please, I notice how hungry and thirsty I am, and I don't stop eating soft fruit till my stomach complains. Late in the day, with many pounds of ripe fruit picked and neatly stored in the refectory pantry, I drink a pint of water and take my leave of the Morisco boys. My guilt about Luis is partially relieved for if he sees me as a friend he'll realise I had nothing to do with his incarceration.

After visiting the latrines, I return to the round tower in the hope of asking the painter Weddesteeg those questions that have been intriguing me. I make my way up to the first-floor studio, but only the monk and the horse remain in the room. The painting stands drying, aired by a breeze drifting through an open window. The shadow on the left of the canvas is unaltered. (So it is to be part of the scene then, the human cavity.)

The monk has his back to me when I enter. He's wearing a painting smock so I guess he must be acting as Weddesteeg's apprentice while the Fleming is resident in the convento. Harmen's brushes have been cleaned and the paint jars sealed. I don't imagine the painter would have

55

done these chores himself. The monk is squatting down in front of the painting, writing something on a piece of parchment. He hasn't heard me come in. Standing and raising his arms to the canvas, he stretches a piece of white thread across the length of the horse. He's taking the horse's measurements, I suppose. I've done this kind of thing myself, with Pacheco's paintings, when I've had to make copies of them.

The monk, wiry and supple, stoops down to the floor again. I decide to leave, but the monk hears my departing footsteps and I'm forced to explain my presence.

'I have a couple of questions for Señor Weddesteeg.'

The monk shakes his head but says considerately. 'He's gone into town. He doesn't take his meals in the refectory.'

'I'll come back another day,' I nod, moving back a few paces, still transfixed by the painting.

'Of course. But don't come tomorrow. Father Rastro has invited the Castle inspectors to view the painting, and they might arrive any time.'

Colour floods my cheeks. Father Rastro's one step ahead of Carlos Zamorana and his invidious spy then. He must have organised the Castle inspection some time back, if it's an official visit.

'Father Rastro's taking every precaution. He knows the painting may prove contentious,' says the monk gravely.

Part of me wants to rush away, and part of me wants to stay and find out more.

'About the buyer . . . ' I begin uncertainly.

'Doña Fillide. A long-time friend of Father Rastro's. And recently a patron of our Order.'

A private buyer, as I imagined. And a foreigner. I'm only surprised that it's a woman.

But then I'm not. Rastro must be attached to Doña Fillide. That's why he's putting himself through this risky charade.

I'm not sure if I can ask the thing I now want to ask. But if the monk's just a Morisco, I can perhaps afford to speak candidly. He seems obliging enough.

'Father Rastro's doing all this for her then?'

The monk doesn't blink. He smiles, and gestures to the painting. 'For that one, he is.'

So it's to be with Paula. She has made fools of us all.

'A wonderful painting,' I say, in parting, feeling I should give it my own stamp of approval.

The monk nods, and says 'I know,' with such confidence (for a minion) that I find it a little disconcerting.

CHAPTER FIVE

At Home with Paula Sánchez

The sun is just beginning to set. I stand in my side-garden and pass a sprig of parsley through an open window to Prospera who reaches out to accept my offering. Decomposing sunlight casts a copper hue; the kitchen walls have turned the burnished colour of the curved tureen in which Violeta is stirring eggs.

Prospera washing parsley. Shaking it dry over-vigorously like she's burnt her hand. Possibly trying to shake off my stare. I loiter at the window, vaguely. Unready to come inside. I see Violeta shake her head at Prospera. Tss. Why is mistress sticking her neck in here? After hours holding my breath in a roomful of men, I crave some female company. Between the strong arms of Violeta and Prospera I float to the surface. Permission to be myself? Not quite. Either hanging in a painting, or leaning against the window frame, I don't quite belong.

Today Diego Velázquez visited us in the convento. Such a surprise to see him there. I didn't find out exactly why he'd come either. Perhaps Father Rastro wanted another opinion on the painting. Diego knows one of the Mercedarian boys, so that may have been his purpose. How tall Diego's grown since those days when I sat for his master. Then I saw him frequently. I still have a flared cape of Diego's that Pacheco lent me to go home in one cold night. I should have returned it, I know, but a man's cape can come in handy. And it has. It'd be too small for Diego now, but perhaps I'll return it anyway.

The light in the kitchen is changing again, dulling the molten gleam of Violeta's exposed elbow as she stands, arm bent, boiling eggs in the watery bouillon. The shutters creak as I press them closed. Walking round the side of the house, I find I'm still clucky about the earth I'm standing on. Paula Sánchez, a property owner! (Bishop Rizi gave me the house, but *I* chose it.)

Take off my transparent manta in the hallway and cross the indoor patio. After doing a loop around my gurgling fountain I perform a little balancing act on the stone rim. On the absent ladder-man's behalf, I say to myself. Star jump down from the rim then rush upstairs inspired. Change out of my convento clothes. The red dress, poor lamentable thing, is fraying at the cuffs and collar. The seams are splitting, but Harmen Weddesteeg says this isn't a problem for the painting. In fact it helps that I look a bit worse for wear. The dress must be sponged clean for tomorrow's sitting. I scent a pan of hot water with ambergris. Dampen a muslin cloth and gently spot the velvet. Handle with care lest thy robe fall apart. Lest thy self fall apart in the process!

I admit to feeling more at home in this Magdalen dress than any I've worn since being a child, those coarse plain frocks my mother stitched, then captured me in. But it's not really the dress, it's the company of Enrique Rastro and Harmen Weddesteeg that nurtures me. It's the men's desultory joking, their mirthful carry-on during the sittings when their clever conversation makes me feel I'm at the theatre, witnessing a comedia. I hope the men are conversing for my benefit, as much as they are for each other. Sometimes I venture an 'oh' or 'ah' of curiosity, but I don't like to expose my ignorance. Listen out for praise, yes. Harmen sheds compliments like a fire sheds sparks. He's always pretending he's lost his sight to me.

'Ah,' he says, leaping down the last five steps of his ladder. 'Where is she, where's my Magdalena?' He covers his eyes with his hand like he's shielding them from the sun.

He flounders about. Stumbles towards me. Harmen takes a quick peek through the shield of his fingers. 'My angel,' he cajoles, stepping back, mouth agape. Am I shooting golden arrows? No, not even penitent, though I'd like to be.

Harmen drinks me up. 'My sight is returned. I only have eyes for you, Paula.'

Once when Harmen climbed down from his loft he was actually wearing a blindfold. Can you believe it? What recklessness! He tripped over a bucket then crawled across the floor towards my amused titter. I couldn't help loving his silliness. He made a big to-do about drawing near and fondling my bare feet. Rising, he patted my veiled head to reassure himself it was really me. Felt the bones of my face, 'Good for sculpture, eh.'

Really? He's too much. Then theatrically pulling his blindfold off. 'Bless you Paula. Blind no longer!'

What a charmer. Anyone who can make me feel that special deserves my affection. Love? It looked like it might go that way for a while. I was attracted to Harmen in the beginning. Probably because I sensed he wouldn't stoop to barter for me. There's that supple time when getting to know another. One is open to the possibility of love. But it went no deeper with him. Or with me, to tell you the truth. It doesn't go deep for me with many men. (A risk of heart seems beyond me.) But Harmen's gregariousness is compelling and he's handsome in that sandy, solid Fleming way. I might have been receptive to something more with him, but I sensed he was privately disapproving. Or unavailable.

He told me straight out one afternoon, 'You've stolen my sight Paula, but you're not going to take my heart.'

I began to doubt my allure. Concentrated on my trade. To kneel silently for two hours takes a lot of fortitude. I have to control my impulse to call it quits or to complain about the pain it causes me to stay kneeling with my head twisted around for such a long time. Father Rastro understands my discomfort, because he's always waiting to help me stand after each protracted sitting. He insists I walk around in the intermissions. He offers me water from a glass that he polishes clean before giving to me. The crystal sparkles in his hand. Then it's sparkling in my hand. The water tasting sweeter than normal.

I've never met a person like Enrique Rastro before. At first I found him rather languid in manner, but more recently I've started thinking of him as serene. He's the same, inside and outside. The outer Enrique appears to live in perfect harmony with the inner, private Enrique. He's a glove and you touch him first on the outside. When you put your hand inside, you find the lining is the same. I've noticed that in the average person there's usually some discordance between the two, but Enrique is a perfect match. This may explain why he's suited to the single life of a friar. A marriage has already taken place, a marriage within himself.

I'm a little starry-eyed about both Harmen and Enrique. On occasion I leave the convento physically exhausted, but mentally refreshed. As I make my way towards the river, I don't notice the acrid smells of dying day, the stench of chamberpots spilled in gutters, the food refuse piled high in laneways. When I cross the bridge the breeze lifts the hem of my gown and twirls the manta round my body. My wings pulse like a bird's. I float free in a wet-dry silver sky.

Having finished cleaning my red dress, I lay it down flat across the base of the closet. (It's too threadbare to hang upon a hook.) There's something I'm looking for. Don't know where I put it. No daylight left to draw upon. I hover in darkness for a moment. In the absence of a reassuring image in a mirror, what aspect of myself have I retained? Just a pulse, my voice and a few threads of language tangled in my head like old necklaces in a jewellery box. Starting out again in a completely dark world I would be both powerless and anonymous; I would have no choice but to seek out the man with the nutcracker. Let the ladder-man water me as he does the neighbours' birds and plants. I would do it for love perhaps; but after the wonder, comes the hurt. Why does the hurt last longer than the wonder?

Was the breaking not meant to happen? Is it against my nature to be broken from?

I'm contemplating love from a new angle tonight. One possibility, I think, is to enter a completely dark world and resort to the primary sensations of taste, touch and smell. Sounds, like the snapping of the nutcracker startle; they remind me of a crackling hearth. There's a tapping nearby. Someone's at the door. It's only Violeta, chiding, 'Señorita, not dressed yet!' I take the proffered candle and she leaves me in peace.

Clinging to the leftover mood from my sojourn in the convento, I remain within my imaginings as my body moves like a wooden toy on a pulley towards my dresser. Observe the candle's red and yellow flickering in the mirror. The flame in the reflection appears to be burning in the middle of my chest, just like the sacred heart. The illusion takes hypnotic hold of me. A soothing voice, 'Let the blue Mary enter your wilting heart. Let the blue Mary heal your red Mary; lay them down, side by side, blue and red.'

I'm familiar with both Marys from my time with the Mercedarians. Enrique Rastro seems to delight in making me bump into every marble statue of the Virgin on our daily circuits round the seminary. Coming in and going out the snow-white Marys preside, plaster robed in sky-bright blue. 'The Virgin will hear your prayers,' Father Rastro encourages, 'She will make you strong in the Lord . . . '

But, I wickedly notice, the convento shelters the Virgin's fallen female friends too. While I'm walking beside Enrique, I'm keeping an eye out for the undergrowth of red Mary Magdalens. They are my secret allies. There's enough russet-gowned penitents hanging about the convento — in tapestries and paintings — to make you really wonder about the priests' sworn allegiance to the Virgin. I can tell you that such impure thoughts regarding the priests have crossed my mind more than once.

I know my conversations between colours on a painter's palette. I've dabbled on a few of these discarded trays in miscellaneous artist's studios. If the blue Mary and the red Mary converge, a violet Mary is born.

Impaled delight! The flame in the mirror, the one that is burning in the middle of my chest, flickers purple in sympathy.

Chilling conversations from the past return to plague me when I'm least expecting them. Baneful influences rise like a soupy river-mist that leaves a stain. A younger me was persuaded to think and act in ways that weren't my own.

'I'll not work as a concubine,' I told some housemother at the age of fourteen.

'A lot of women prefer it to marriage,' was the tart reply.

Why did the Christians I worked for never say it was a sin to sell my body? It wasn't *my* fault I took the wrong path. Lots of women were selling their physical wares and lots of men clamouring to buy them. Yet I could have done worse. I might have ended up in the brothel with Hortense. A year after the fateful dust-storm separated us I encountered my village friend in a marketplace.

'They keep us clean. A doctor checks for disease. And the brothel padre doesn't make us rent our towels and sheets,' Hortense said, both prickly and proud.

And what if the doctor *finds* symptoms of the French pox? I thought in horror. What then?

No-one has ever made me wear the yellow head-covering, the mark of the prostitute, on the streets. I can call myself a courtesan. I have held my head high, gone into grand homes, sat among ladies whose ruffs were so broad they made the wearers look like giant sun-flowers. And I've never caught the abominable disease. While I'm holding a parasol with Bishop Rizi's emblem embroidered on it, no Jesuit's going to tap me on the shoulder, bridle me in a yellow noose and pull me inside the Magdalen house. On the twenty-second of July, the feast of Mary Magdalen, rather than sensibly hiding away indoors as Bishop Rizi makes me promise to do, I'm overcome by a gnawing curiosity to go into town and look upon the repenting whores. I hasten to Saint Peter's, stand on pilgrims' rise and watch the procession of polluted women in yellow scarves filing into the cathedral. I'm fascinated and vindicated by the sheer volume of women: 'If scores of them do it, I can't be so bad.' A part of me yearns to follow in their wake. A part of me does join them in spirit.

I ignore the jeering crowd on pilgrims' rise. The yellow women deserve our pity not our scorn. I get calloused hands from scratching bits of the skin on my palms while awaiting the penitents' reappearance. How I envy their sisterhood, the way they exit the cathedral in rows with arms linked and heads held high. Purified, forgiven and privately sanctioned to sin again. Father Rastro has encouraged me to join the procession this year. 'It would do you good to go, Paula.' But to be herded inside and forced to confess before the flagellating mystics might make me feel worse, not better. I've told Father Rastro I'm still making up my mind. I cannot lie. But I cannot tell him the truth either. When the day comes around I won't be there with the women in yellow.

Pulling open a dresser drawer I take out my make-up case. I barely notice my face in the mirror as I pat the powder on. You can only look at your face if your face consents to be looked at. There are so many people pulling on me, telling me what to think and what to do. Earlier in the afternoon the normally tolerant Harmen Weddesteeg was having his say: 'Turn a bit more to the right, Paula. And keep still, won't you.' Even the ladder-man wants me to be something else, to become a circus performer for him. I can't think to what purpose I could put the skill of standing on a ladder unsupported. Falling into balance is a futile enterprise.

But I can pull myself out of lassitude. Think of my mother once upon a time. When I was about three I swallowed a pearl. It is my first memory. Mama said it would come out of my bottom, but after her searching and pouring water on my faeces, no pearl was found. 'You have a pearl inside you now,' said Mama with a worried smile. I liked the idea of Mama's pearl living inside me. I expected it to pop out of my naval if I ate too much. That pearl is probably still inside me, worn small by the constant washing of corrosive juices, a tiny seed-pearl sewn into the lining of my stomach. When I get a tummy-ache I imagine this may be the cause. With Mama I ate a pearl and didn't die. With Mama there was happiness and happiness, and then there was nothing.

Descant chimes interrupt my thoughts. Violeta hastens to answer the front door. It's too late to dress for Guido Rizi. I'll receive him in my oriental dressing gown. Tonight I have a particular reason for wanting him to arrive, and soon. I smile brazenly at myself in the mirror, rub a thin layer of wax across my lips to make them gleam, then pick up my candle-end and hurry downstairs.

The Bishop is wearing a civilian frockcoat rather than his religious robes, but I only notice what he's holding in his hand. A parcel wrapped in brown paper. I take the gift and loosen the string. Inside is a tall bottle containing a medicinal balsam. 'The witch hazel balsam,' Guido Rizi informs me solemnly in his deep gravelly voice, as if he's saying 'the son of God', or something sacred. I secrete a smile. From my frequent complaints, he knows that some time after a painting session the agony sets in. Lately I've been using this as an excuse to avoid intimacy with him.

I open the bottle and sniff the liquid. It smells pleasantly of myrrh and Mecca balsam. Guido Rizi offers to rub the substance on my neck and knees, but I excuse myself to perform this function behind a painted screen, the latter another acquisition from the Orient. As Guido purchased the screen for me, he will be happy to see me using it. And he is.

I start to massage the aching lower regions of my neck and some of the pain instantly subsides. 'I could do a lot worse,' I'm thinking. 'I've done a lot worse. It is not his fault that I find him so unattractive.'

Later, naked and on my back with my legs spread apart, it feels as if a plucked quail is being forced inside my vagina.

The skin of the meat is cold and loose, the bones frail, crushable. My penetrator is not unclean, but he smells like someone who's just died. Guido Rizi's odour is curiously sexless. I bury my face in the feather bolster. Pretend I'm elsewhere. Back in the convento, scratching like a cat at the paling of the Cross.

When it's over, I leave Rizi's side, and lie down on a pile of cushions on the floor. But tonight sleep escapes me even when I'm lying yards from his reach. If I concentrate hard I can levitate myself onto the rooftops. Soon I'm in the sweet, metal-clacking company of the ladder-man, wondering if he's really mute or just pretending.

'Having mastered the skill of falling into balance,' I'm explaining to myself, 'the ladder-man begins to teach me the art of expressing love without speaking.'

I borrow the ladder-man's chalk, draw a square and write the number four inside of it. He draws a square on top, using one of my lines as one of his, and inside his square he writes the number two. I know what I'm supposed to do. Write a 'one' above the two. We're falling into a second childhood. That's the nicest thing about romance, at least at the start when there are whole territories still to be discovered in each other, the mapping just beginning, just like Christopher Columbus setting out from Spain — the bright steel of childhood intensity returns.

On the floor in my bedchamber, sleep tucks me in. But when I'm asleep I dream in black and white. Harmen is in my dream and he's crying because his beautiful painting has been leached of colour. I grind awake like a ship coming into dock, lying on the floor with a dead hand caught under me. How I hate the feel of my dead hand, the cold, floppy horror of it. Then the sharp needles as the dead hand comes back to life.

I roll onto my back and wait for the chatter of birds and the trundle of barrels along the street that signal a clean, new day. A clean new day will be happening across the river in San Vicente too. In the Mercedarian convento, timekeepers and sacristans will be scuttling through the darkness, feet crunching on snails. Priests do not remember their dreams, they do not: bells waken them in the fullness of sleep. Some priests though, dislike a rude awakening. Enrique Rastro would be one of these, I suppose. I picture him sliding gracefully out of bed, woken by his internal bell, neatly folding away his dreams beneath his pillow. Now he's walking down to the latrines, a lantern in his hand exposing swollen ankles. Morning dew on his feet, a morning prayer at his lips a minnow ascending to Heaven.

I imagine him filling a basin with water for shaving, and lathering his face and neck with slow measured strokes. His brush makes a half-ellipse around his face and his face is held at the very centre of the oval mirror. First light filtering through the lattice patterns silver lace at his cheek and throat. He hasn't cut himself for as long as he can remember. He puts down his razor and runs his hand over his chin, pink but for the blackheads of finest stubble. In silent contemplation Enrique Rastro would be deliberating his schedule for the day. It is his ruling quality. Careful deliberation. Strength of purpose.

Yesterday I arrived at the convento a little early. I'd been running to get there, believing I was late. An orderly led me to the Major courtyard where I found the Mercedarian leader sitting on a bench reading the Holy Scriptures. Enrique inclined his head when he saw me coming. Stayed seated. Motivated not by rudeness, but by doubt or shyness. I'm guessing that Enrique is unversed in sexual affairs. That's sad for a man of forty. Some priests in Seville *do* take their vows of chastity seriously. (But most, believe me, do not.)

Eventually Enrique closed the book and rose from the bench. We had a brief conversation about nothing. We were interrupted by some raised voices. Two men were gesticulating in front of a lone plum tree on the other side of the courtyard. Enrique shook his head but his expression remained mild. He predicted he'd be called over to adjudicate, and in a moment he was. The old tree, we were told by the building supervisor when we arrived on the scene, needed to be chopped down to make room for an ornamental pond. The argument was over the fate of a bird's nest lodged in the branches.

'If we remove the nest, the mother will disown her chicks. The little birds will die,' pleaded the other man, a monk.

'I've been waiting a month to cut down this tree, all because of you,' the building supervisor complained, frowning at the skinny monk.

Enrique looked from one to the other. Then he climbed the ladder and inspected the nest for himself. The chicks were squawking. I couldn't see their mother. Perhaps she'd already flown away..

Enrique stood with his head basted in leaves. His expression was so benign I thought he must have decided against taking any action. Then plums were shaking and leaves were rustling. Enrique had reached over and pulled the nest out of the fork of branches. It didn't come away easily; it took some effort. I watched him climb back down the tree, cradling the nest with its noisy occupants against his breast. When Enrique was standing beside me again, I noticed his fingers and wrists were badly scratched. He didn't seem aware of these cuts. He was looking at the monk whose name I do not know or haven't bothered to remember. It is the same monk who's in the painting

The Penitent Woman. He was staring at the place in the branches where the bird's nest had just been. Enrique offered the bird's nest to the monk, but the young man didn't seem to comprehend what was intended. Enrique turned blankly to the building supervisor and gave him the go-ahead to cut down the tree.

We took the bird's nest with its shrill occupants to the round tower with us. Enrique kept asking the monk if he'd like to look after the chicks, but the monk seemed not to hear. The birds were making a lot of fuss. It was going to be hard to concentrate through the sitting. Diego Velázquez seems to like birds. He told us about a goldfinch he owned that reliably woke him at dawn every day. He attempted to warble a few distinctive notes, in imitation. Diego can hold a tune it seems.

I wasn't surprised when Harmen Weddesteeg complained about the hatchlings. Enrique got up from the sitting and gave the nest to Diego to look after. It was lucky Diego turned up today, and that Enrique is so merciful. The chicks will probably die, he said, but we'll keep them comfortable until they do.

The more time I spend with the ladder-man, the more Enrique Rastro appears in my thoughts. And vice-versa. I sense these two beings are connected in some way. I come home from the convento thinking about how kind Enrique is, and the ladder-man appears like a phantom on a distant rooftop. I go to sleep dreaming of the ladder-man and wake up thinking about Enrique. I fall asleep remembering the touch of Enrique and wake up in the ladder-man's arms. They are like two plants growing within a single clay pot; one plant will fade as the other thrives. But I'm not sure which is to fade and which is to thrive. One occupies my afternoons, the other my early evenings. They are both love secrets. A secret from each other, of course, and also secrets I'm keeping from the world. And what of Guido Rizi? He is my official gift-giving benefactor who keeps me from penury and social scorn. For the last half year I've believed that the time I spend with him can be poured down the drain like his urine from my chamberpot after he leaves. That I can scrub the chamberpot clean and be none the worse. That half of the day I live and the other half I must die and that this is the natural order of things for a woman like me.

Having eventually fallen asleep well after dawn, it's mid-morning when I can finally bear to wake up. Bishop Rizi's already departed, as I'd intended. It's the city that wakes me. The city is singing as church bells resound the fifth hour of the day. Yellow shields clash in the windows of belfries. Bells swing like clusters of golden pears. Babies wake: the dying revive. In Triana, my ginger cat Maio is scratching at the balcony hatch, wanting to come inside.

I listen to him scratch. 'Shut the bells up,' I mutter.

Maio is unfaithful; I've seen him accept purred invitations from other cats, and curd from strangers. I get up to open the hatch and he comes down the stairs wonkily, as though crippled. Must have fallen asleep in a Triana belfry to lose his balance like this. He slouches into the darkness and softness of my closet. I salvage my red velvet pelt from beneath his paws and throw the robe over my shoulder. I must dress to go to the convento. But I sit down on my bed for a moment, my hands kneading the crushed velvet. It's some kind of primitive ritual, this kneading, the dark oil flowing out of me. I won't have to think about Bishop Rizi for several days, and I'm not going to think about him until I absolutely have to.

When I have the Magdalen dress laced and fresh powder on, I stand at the window. A partial view of Seville is available to me from this height. For a full view, I would have to go up on my balcony, but for now I merely want to collect my thoughts and ponder the prevailing weather. Are clouds heading Seville's way? Nothing in sight, but it usually pours some time in the afternoon.

I picture myself in the near future, making my way across Triana Bridge. I'm in control of the afternoon ahead, and everything will happen of my own volition. I notice, to my dismay, the glass I'm looking through needs cleaning.

Dead insects are crushed on the outside of the pane. I don't have a clear view of the world after all.

I bought this pane of glass a year ago at great expense. A carpenter removed the oiled parchment and inserted the square into the existing wooden frame. It's made a huge difference, having daylight flooding into my bedchamber, being able to look out and see a mosaic of sky whenever I want. I particularly love waking when it's fully light; the sun buzzing around me. When I wipe the particles of sleep from the corners of my eyes I find not grit, but pollen on my fingertips.

Turning from the window I wonder what Enrique and Harmen would do if I didn't turn up this afternoon. What if I fell ill and had to stop working for them? How would they react? The thought of letting them down or of missing out on my own pleasure makes me nauseous. It's within my control to bring a halt to the painting of *The Penitent Woman* and to end the relationships that are forming around me. What if it *did* happen, if fate intervened, or if I lost my confidence and didn't go in search of auspicious company this afternoon?

But I'm just imagining my absence in the convento. I'm going to arrive on time as I always do. And if by some unlucky chance I do fall sick with a tertian ague, Harmen and Rastro could make do without me. The painting is nearing completion anyway; it will soon be finished.

Skipping downstairs, I slow to saunter through the indoor patio, listening to the agile water spilling from the fountain. At the coat stand near the door I unhook my tulle manta, slip it on and tie a bow beneath my chin. The umbrella is standing upright below the other coats, but I don't reach in and pull it out. I decide to take a risk.

CHAPTER SIX

Stealth and More Stealth

In which Diego Velázquez relates another adventure at the top of the Giralda

On Sundays I sleep over with my family in San Pedro. We meet up after Mass, and from that moment on, I have no peace. My little brothers are jumping on me, my mother pampering me with so much food you'd think my master starves me, and my sisters teasing me about Juana Pacheco. I love all the attention I get, I don't mind lying on the floor and the boys pouncing on me and I enjoy being able to say whatever comes into my head, but I hate the girls' insults about Juana Pacheco. 'Is *she* the bride for you?' they smirk, and I want to throttle them. I'd almost not come home to avoid these insults.

Monday morning and I'm leaving the house in darkness when I remember I've forgotten my goldfinch. I go back inside and grab the cage I've left by my makeshift pallet. The bird punctures my dreams before dawn with a reliable, '*te*llit, *te*llit, *te*llit'. Its pretty silvery tinkling is worth waking up to: '*te*llit, *te*llit, *te*llit'. I bought the finch, not for its song, but for its red face, buff flanks and yellow wings. God in his heavenly workshop must be painting these beauties with his genius paintbrush every day, then letting them flutter straight down to earth.

I unlatch the front door of my family home, carrying my goldfinch with me this time. My master and I are working on a Greco–Roman ceiling in the Casa de Pilatos: 'The gods of antiquity,' with all pagan motifs removed. I'm going there directly, rather than to Pacheco's. The streets of San Pedro are asleep, except for some singing drunks returning from taverns. These crooners keep losing their balance. I can't fathom why people would enjoy being so out of control.

Recently I've been passing Catarina de Loyola's house at every opportunity, though I always cast my face down so no-one watching might guess my interest. I'm passing Catarina's place right now and, because it's dark, I stare up at the windows. When you pass a house you look at the windows first. As if it's a face and you're looking at a person's eyes that can tell you so much. Up on the first floor of the Loyola residence, someone's awake. A curtain flushes rose-pink then parts open. A face at the window holding a candle-end; she's only visible for a moment but I'm sure it's her. The curtain falls back into place, turns grey. She's blown out her candle. Not long after, I hear a rattle and the gate onto the street clicks open. I lunge behind a date palm so I won't be seen.

Catarina emerges in a hooded cloak, veiled like a Moor. Her apparel is not so unusual. Sevillian women usually veil their faces when they go out alone, so they won't be recognised and perhaps chastised. In fact, if a woman is veiled it usually means she's up to no good. The Church has tried to stop the wearing of veils but the decrees are only observed for six months, then our female folk go back to their furtive ways. The authorities can't arrest half the women of the town, can they? Catarina looks around anxiously, ducks her head like a squirrel, then moves off in a northerly direction. I pull my feathered hat low over my brow and follow at a discreet distance, clutching my goldfinch cage in my left hand.

Catarina's heading towards the open fields beyond the old walls. I consider turning back to the House of Pilatos, but my dutiful side is powerless in the face of my attraction to the girl.

She's slowing down and comes to a halt outside the large, gracious home of Fillide Rosano. I shield myself behind a lemon tree. Through the scratching leaves I see that Catarina has taken cover too. She's crouching behind a pedlar who's fast asleep on his cushioned barrow. Catarina and I are only ten yards apart, the consoling darkness a thread pulled tight between us.

We've not been waiting long when someone comes through the Rosano gateway. It's young Marius, heir to the Rosano fortune. (It's his Genoese mother, Doña Fillide, who commissioned the Weddesteeg painting in the Mercedarian convento.) A leather bag slung over his shoulder, Marius doesn't glance about to see what the night is storing in its gloom. He hurries off into town. Catarina gives him a head start then springs up from her shelter. I shadow the girl, clutching the goldfinch cage in my left hand, wanting her to remain just out of touch so she can stay my fantasy.

Off in the distance, Marius is striding along and soon he starts running as though he's late for an appointment. Catarina and I are falling behind. When Marius enters the maze of Santa Cruz it's harder still to trace him. Is he trying to lose Catarina? I'm guessing he's on a pre-dawn mission that doesn't involve the girl. But she obviously has a singular interest in him.

I'm concentrating so hard on keeping in touch with

Catarina while remaining out of sight, that I don't realise how close we've come to the cathedral until it's looming right overhead. I look up in fright. In the dark, the cathedral bears the appearance of a steep, overhanging mountain. I follow Catarina round the side of the building. Here the giant portals are open for dawn prayer. Light billows onto the street: the lambent haze of a thousand flickering candles.

Catarina slides back her hood and veil and enters the sacred building. I take off my hat and once inside, lurk near the entrance, encumbered by the goldfinch cage which is resting on my left hip. (The clergy won't like me bringing my bird in here.)

Nuns and priests are converging on the high altar from all directions. They're mumbling prayers, creating a buzzing drone. It both looks and sounds like a giant beehive with the Queen bee presiding at the massive twelve-yard-high altarpiece. Thousands of dancing candles are melting her golden combs.

Catarina, standing in the central aisle, is obstructing the file of persons moving towards the gilded altar. But the clergy have the air of sleepwalkers about them and don't seem to notice the strange girl hovering in their midst. I wish she'd move on though; she'll cause an accident if she doesn't watch out.

I can see Marius hurrying along the shadowy cloisters on the other side of the nave. He's stopping at the entrance to the Giralda. Talking to the sacristan at the gate. It looks as if he's handing the sacristan some money. Then he enters the tower precinct and is gone from sight.

Catarina must have spotted him. She's on the move again. Crossing the cathedral in the direction of the tower gate. Here she unfastens her cloak and takes out her purse. After a brief consultation with the sacristan, she too enters the Giralda.

I could see it happening, but still I'm furious. I want to pounce on the pair and spoil their fun. I search my pockets for a coin. None is to be found, but the sacristan looks familiar. Here's my chance.

My friendly chat works, and I'm following Catarina and Marius up the Giralda rampway, my goldfinch cage knocking against my left thigh. I've energy to burn it seems; the climb has never been easier. There's a single oil lamp at every floor, otherwise I'm ascending in the dark. I'm so spurred on I feel I can see in the dark. I know I've almost reached the minaret on the thirty-fifth floor when the windows narrow. A lantern reveals Catarina perched at the top of the steps, but I can only see the lower portion of her body.

She moves off the highest stone and disappears into the

minaret. I leave my birdcage at the base of the steps and climb up after her. When I reach the top and peer out into the night I can't see a thing except for the stars. The minaret is unlit, the sky a chimney swilling sparks.

Catarina's crouching in the shadows of the belfry, about twenty feet away, with her back to me. I had no idea a grown girl could scrunch herself up to be quite that small. A timid, nocturnal creature, terrified and hypnotised by her quarry. I decide my best bet is to go round the other way. Then I will be able to see what Marius is up to, and avoid a confrontation with Catarina. What would be the worst scenario? To find Marius undressing perhaps. But he'd not risk that on Holy ground. I crawl on my hands and knees along the cold hard floor and lament the indignity of being in love. When I reach the final curve I rise and sidle around the stone ledge.

A young man is standing a fair way off, at the edge of the balcony. In his hands he's holding a lightweight telescope. His head is tilted back and he's looking at the sky. A breeze is messing his hair, making it drift about his neck and shoulders. Marius peruses the constellations with gentle deflections and swirls of the raised telescope. He's sniffling a little, which dissolves my pride and makes me compassionate. This youth, etched against the night-sky, might be myself, or a brother or someone else I could care about unconditionally as a close friend. I begin to doubt that a rendezvous between Marius and Catarina is imminent. I even wonder if they have more than a slight acquaintance with each other. Perhaps Marius is to Catarina, what Catarina is to me.

While I'm waiting for Catarina to appear at Marius's side, I notice the youth is wearing a green doublet. If I'm able to see colours again the dark must be thinning. If the sun is about to rise I'm going to be very late for work. Pacheco will be arriving at the Casa de Pilatos before me. I turn and tip-toe back the way I came, just in time to observe Catarina in her flowing cloak descending the open portal ahead of me. She's holding her shoes in one hand, so as not to be heard, I suppose. I edge backwards, giving her time to be on her way.

Did she come here to look at the stars with Marius and then change her mind? But Marius wasn't expecting her. He seems oblivious to her interest. I feel a surge of confidence and decide to catch Catarina up, but at the moment I'm about to navigate the steps, a sacristan materialises below and begins his upward climb. When he reaches the top, he sees me waiting to go down and grabs hold of me.

'Come on, young fellow. You can give me a hand with the big bell. I'm on my own this morning.'

'But my bird!' I say in concern, peering down the steps

in search of the cage that I've just remembered. The sacristan has no interest in birds. He grips my arm and we move deeper into the belfry. Here the sacristan shows me how to execute the ropes. He hands me some wax for my ears. Then, together, we begin to pull a couple of the mighty bells, up and down.

As the crash of heavy metal shakes the morning awake I'm thinking I could really hurt myself doing this. If a bell swings the wrong way it could knock me over. I could end up headless. This is not a musical instrument, it's closer to cannon-fire.

Finally the task is over, but not before I've thought my arms were going to be ripped off my body. I jump down from the belfry and wander about in a daze, no longer caring who sees me up here. When my head stops throbbing, I take a proper look around. Marius has disappeared, presumably alarmed by the wounding bells or having finished his contemplation of the galaxies. The eastern horizon is beginning to smoulder and the stars look a lot like red stigmata in the vapid, receding dark.

Out on the street again, and without my goldfinch cage, I run all the way to the Casa de Pilatos. Having come so close to the object of my desire, my feelings for Catarina seem to have survived the encounter. But there is a new, unsettling suspicion about her, and about Marius too.

After doing my penance with the bells, I discovered my goldfinch cage wasn't at the bottom of the steps where I left it. One of those two must have stolen my bird, and the loss is a great grief to me.

'Do you know Marius Rosano?' I ask Pacheco, after I've made up for being late by working assiduously all morning. I must have spoken too lightly and my master hasn't heard. 'Rosano is interested in astronomy,' I speak more loudly this time. Pacheco stops painting and looks across at me.

'Have you been reading my mind again?' Pacheco shifts into a less precarious position on the scaffolding. 'You may have an opportunity to discuss astronomy with young Rosano in the future. His mother has been sojourning in Genoa and she's organising a party to celebrate her return.'

We'll be going to Marius's place soon then. Things often happen like that, I've noticed. You're thinking about someone, you hardly know them, and then they start turning up in your life with inexplicable frequency.

CHAPTER SEVEN

Paula Receives an Enticing Invitation

The wind is swaying; the skies are full of loose feathers and distraught birds. Perched on my roof, I see flying geese juddering in the gusty tumult. On the streets below quill-makers are running about, attempting to catch the multitude of feathers wafting down.

The sky is jam-packed tonight, that's for sure. With their wings stretched sail-taut behind them, witches loft skyward, away from the dry tinder of papal judgement. Gunpowder sneezes: the sky fills with white puffballs and fizzy red flares. Across the river in cathedral quarter, Carlos Zamorana, with a loaded arquebus, will be trying to shoot the creepy black women out of the sky. Carlos Zamorana, who, I imagine, loathes nothing more intensely than the thought of a witch's sagging breasts and wizened paps.

But only the little birds fall. Plop, plop, plop, onto the bare-breasted balconies of Seville. Blood-spattered birds, frightening children and disturbing cats. (Maio the Fraught is hiding under my skirt.)

While the wind is having its say, sandblasting Seville like a run-amok orator, I force my way (the wind flaying my hair) over to the ladder-man's shelter. My nutcracker man has something important to show me tonight. Inside his tin shed he's holding a sheet of thick paper under a lantern. Moths stick to the honey-coloured parchment and I brush them away. I lean closer to the paper and moths land on my face. The ladder-man is pressing close and I can see that he actually does shave that youthful skin (this man could even grow a beard if he wanted to). This thought arouses me no end. As I sound out the words on the paper the ladder-man is nodding instructively. What I'm reading is an invitation from the so-called 'ladder-men's guild' to a so-called 'ladder-men's ball'. All the ladder-men in Seville will be there. They can each take one ladder and one guest along, but not more than one of each. Have I read it right? Yes, I have. Oh la-di-da. A ladder-man ball! I had been to nothing so fanciful since I was seven. And only one day to wait.

To get to the gala ball we have to cross the river because

the event is to be held on one of the biggest galleries of Seville, the magnificent upper deck of the Casa de Pilatos. My ladder-man's agitated about having to go down onto the streets to passage over there. He writes on his slate that he hasn't stepped on land for years. He's not comfortable around streets and horses, I remember. He must have got his hand caught in a drain when he was a little boy, or maybe his mother carried him around on her hip for far too long and he needs to be airborne to feel content. I hire a carriage to make it easier for him, and he jumps from my house onto the roof of the carriage then climbs into the vehicle through the window. His skinniness helps with this. I tie both our ladders onto the roof with Violeta's and Prospera's assistance. The ladder-man crouches inside the carriage biting his nails.

As soon as we cross the river we seize our ladders and climb back up onto the rooftops again, proceeding to our destination by an up-and-down-slow-and-circuitous route, as though we are scaling a mountain. Normally I'd protest, but I like being with the ladder-man and the more time I get to spend with him the better. We're not known on the proper side of town, and we get quite a barrage of insults and even soft fruit thrown at us for our trespasses. 'We're on our way to the ladder-men's ball,' I proudly explain to the balcony residents and they say, 'Well what do you think the roads are made for?' or 'Yeah, yeah, that's what they all say.'

We meet lots of other ladder-men going the same way, all fountain fresh with wet hair, nicely spruced up and wearing white linen shirts rather than their customary drab shepherd tunics. Their tailored legs and hips are on display as a consequence, but I only have eyes for my svelte ladder-man.

As I've already told you, the ladder-man's ball will take place on the upper gallery of the Casa de Pilatos, not in the great hall. People think that a ladder-man would only want to relax on a rooftop at night. That is a very patronising assumption. It's like offering to take a Turkish guest to the Arabic baths to relax.

'Why aren't we going into the grand hall?' I ask, for that room is magnificent and has a painting of myself 'playing' Susannah on the wall which I'd like to show the ladder-man. I've been in the great hall before, on the arms of many grandées.

But the usher welcoming us onto the gallery says that the Duque de Alcalá — currently sojourning in Madrid — has granted permission for only the gallery to be used for the ladder-men's exploits. And, while the revellers are having fun, the Duke wants all his plants watered too.

But why is the Duke giving up his stately home to

such riff-raff as us? The ladder-men's guild is not even an officially recognised guild, I've been told. It has no legal status. The Duke, the usher tells us, owes a debt to a ladder-man who saved his young son's life. Just in the nick of time, so the story goes, the ladder-man appeared from nowhere and stopped the little boy flying off the roof like the bird he imagined himself to be.

'I will give you anything you want, but not money or furniture,' the Duke promised the swift-footed hero.

'I would have a party for all the long-suffering, blighted ladder-men of Seville,' said the rescuer.

'You will have your party and the best musicians, food and drink on offer,' replied the Duke. The clause about watering the plants came later.

The usher parts a festive sash and we are welcomed onto the spacious upper gallery, already thick with munching, swilling ladder-folk. Some hold goblets, others chicken drumsticks, others watering cans, but I don't see any ladders in their midst. We are invited to leave our ladders standing upright against a wall. I put my ladder next to my ladder-man's. There are dozens of ladders already stacked up here, one in front of the other. They will get mixed up surely, I say to my ladder-man, who answers me by writing on the back of the invitation with a goose-quill, 'A ladder-man always knows his own ladder.' Well, no doubt that's true, but what's to stop a ladder-man coveting another man's property?

The ladder-man smiles and shows me a ticket with the number 629 on it which he puts in a pocket of his beautiful breeches that are just like the ones that Harmen Weddesteeg wears. In fact, I may have borrowed these from Harmen for the night, I can't remember. I borrowed them from somewhere, but all the edges of things are a bit blurry in the ladder-man's world.

Ladder-men are loners; few have brought guests with them and few know each other, except by distant sight, from their time spent on the rooftops. I guess they see each other as competition. This hardly matters tonight though, as they are here in large numbers to eat and drink. But this party is quiet as far as parties go. After a while the guests loosen up and begin to converse with each other and to dance to the little orchestra of viols and clavichord hiding in the wings. Because they have no partners some of the ladder-men go fetch their ladders and dance holding onto these. They do look funny whisking their ladders around as though they are skeletal wives. They may very well have wives at home that they're dreaming of. It'd be nice to think they do.

I look at my ladder-man to see if he wants to dance with me, but he seems contented watching the frivolities and sipping cider. Does he miss his ladder? Every now and then I see him keeping an eye on it. 'I hope *my* ladder doesn't go for a wander,' I say to him in sympathy. The ladder-man puts his arm around me, but I can feel he's not comfortable doing this. He's searching for a grip or a rung, but there's just my spongy body and his hand keeps slipping off my shoulder. Eventually he gives up and goes and fetches his ladder. He seems to be much more content holding onto his ladder than he was holding onto me. I fight back disappointment, but then everything fixes up pretty quickly and he's leaning the ladder against me and we've both got our arms looped through the rungs and my hand is pressing against his sweaty palm. Soon his arms are about my waist and even slipping inside my clothes; as long as we have the ladder propped between us my ladder-man's prepared to be quite adventurous.

The guild leader, a ladder-man called Alonso, is organising a series of contests for us guests. First there will be a race across the adjoining rooftops. Ten men opt to take part. Guild leader Alonso whistles 'Go!' and off the men leap, clutching their ladders. While I stand watching and laughing and eventually clapping the winner, I notice that a couple of ladder-men in the chase are missing limbs. Maybe this is why they have had to become ladder-men. The ladder is like having an extra arm or leg, isn't it? These men are plucky, I admit, to be dashing about the rooftops with parts missing.

The winner gets a bronze statuette of a man hanging upside down on a ladder. Half his luck. Next there's a competition to see who can balance on a ladder for the longest time. I nudge my ladder-man forward. He should try this one. Someone behind me pushes past and drags my ladder-man off to join the line-up of hopefuls. My ladder-man's snared for the competition against his will, and the chosen six climb onto their ladders and we're standing around getting bored as we wait and wait for one of them to fall. These men have attained the art of perfect balance. Not even a tornado would knock one down. Alonso, the guild leader, gets impatient and orders his helpers to apply the under-arm tickles and the balancing men go wobbly and tip over in hysterics. My ladder-man is the last man standing because tickles can't make him laugh. His lips are stuck fast in a purse. He wins a short sharp knife, but he looks horrified when he opens the leather sheath and he passes the knife straight over to me. (My ladder-man is too gentle to own a knife.) But Violeta will be pleased to receive this for her kitchen armoury. I may even keep it for myself.

Then there is 'the best ladder' award and all the ladders are spread out and admired. We vote on a winner. A man with a miraculously extending ladder wins the prize. His ladder pulls in two but my favourite is actually a stripy painted ladder that glows in the dark. Now for the best women's ladder. I discover that there are just three females in the crowd. I hope my ladder will win because I'd love the prize. I would get my ladder engraved by a wood artist for free. But alas, a ladder-woman with a ladder in the shape of a curvaceous female torso wins the prize. This ladder-woman looks a lot like her ladder. She receives smutty jokes and hooting from the crowd when she collects her award.

I go up to congratulate her and we stare at each other as we clasp hands.

'Paula?'

'Hortense!'

It is my friend from the village whom I've not seen for ten years since the day she told me she'd been snared for the brothel. How she has grown. We have a lot to catch up on. After seven years, she tells me, she escaped the brothel with the help of a ladder-man, would you believe. It is a familiar story then, for we women of soiled cloth.

'And you?' she says. 'Look at your beautiful gown, the jewels in your hair. Did you hire these things? Are you truly a ladder-woman?'

I can see she will hate me if I admit that I am not one of the mock-up guild, so I pretend that I am, but she says she's heard tales of my soaring courtesan career, and she lunges forward and scoops up my skirt to denounce me.

'Look at that pitiful, undeveloped calf muscle,' she almost spits.

Just as expected, exposed as a fraud. Well I've certainly got bigger calf muscles than I used to have. I didn't think they were really that pathetic.

'You're an imposter,' she proclaims, and then I wonder if jealousy isn't at the core of all relationships between women.

I run back to my ladder-man sobbing and tell him I'm ready to go home. But I don't want a protracted climb over the roofs of Seville to Triana. I tell my ladder-man I'll just slip downstairs and find my own way out a door onto the street. I'll walk home alone if he doesn't mind; I know my way out of this Casa.

But my ladder-man has other plans for me tonight. He may be mute but he's very directive in his own way. Besides, we're not allowed to exit through the lower quarters of the palace. We have to go back the way we've come in, up and over. I follow him as he climbs from the gallery onto the mansion roof, and together we make our way slowly across the stables and farm buildings to where the Duque de Alcalá's ample orchard begins. Our ladders help us cross from an acorn tree to an almond tree and then we swing into the embrace of a plum tree that has a wooden tree-house nesting among its foliage. An unlocked wooden door hangs on a broken hinge. Once I'm inside the house the ladder-man shifts the door back into its frame.

'You've stayed here before?' I ask.

I imagine him nodding.

'Insects,' I say, looking at the rug on the floor warily.

He throws his handsome doublet (also belonging to Harmen Weddesteeg, I think) across the rug.

'I'm hot,' I say, while I'm really thinking, 'Take my dress off.'

Instinctively, he does. Unwinds my laces. Hook after hook after hook. The swamp of my dress stretches out across the dank rug.

I lie down on my back and he pulls his shirt off and lies down on top of me and puts his hands on my breasts and kisses me, his lips soft but compressed. I kiss him back and try to stick my tongue in his mouth but he keeps his lips firmly closed. Then he moves his mouth away from mine and kisses my neck and pulls my chemise down so he can kiss my breasts. I can feel the heat coming out of his body; he smells of yeast and sugar egg. God loves me, I think, as I open my legs and press my crotch hard up against his groin, wanting to feel his arousal and relieved when I do. He isn't missing anything in that regard.

When I thrust against him, taking such liberties, he presses himself harder too, and then reaches down and pulls my underclothing and stockings away from my body so that I'm completely naked down there.

He doesn't touch me between the legs. Not yet. With one hand he caresses my breasts. The other he runs up and down my legs, then along the inside of my thighs. He's done this to women before, I can tell. He's not as chaste as I imagined. It hardly matters. Maybe it's better he knows a thing or two about women's bodies. He strokes my belly, reaching down to the place where my pubic hair encroaches. His fingers are in my pubic hair now, delving lower and lower.

He doesn't touch my crotch, not yet. Maybe he doesn't intend to either. I'm half expecting he's going to get up and dash outside for the security of his ladder, and then maybe even jerk himself off (privately and pantingly) against one of my lady-ladder's smooth stakes.

But he loosens his breeches (those on loan from Harmen Weddesteeg have never been put to better use) and in the dark I can see his erection pointing up at me. He's a man for sure. It always comes as a surprise to see such bold expressiveness, the pointing penis. This one is vulnerable, not predatory. I can tell the difference. For once I can. He's trembling and his sex is giving off a newborn-baby, wheaten smell; I know I will have no trouble putting this man's penis in my mouth. Not now though. Later. Maybe even later tonight. It must be love if I'm ready to do that. I reach out for him but he pulls my hand away. He'll come if I do that. He lies on his side so his stiff penis is pressing against my thigh and I will him to touch me between the legs.

And he does. Puts his hand inside a glove of warm fluid. Rests there for a moment, then he pushes my legs apart and leans forward to press his mouth against the folds of my sex. I hold his head in my hands and feel like crying. My sex is his, it would seem. I'm about to cry, but the tears choke inside me and won't come out. This is a ladder-man, remember. He's ethereal: sometimes no more than a trick of the light or a nuzzle of river-damp air.

I hear a soft creaking sound nearby; it must be the tree ticking, it is the heartbeat of the tree we're lying up against. When I was a child I thought that each tree had a heart inside its trunk.

The ladder-man lifts his head and I can see he is all too real. He begins stroking me down there until it becomes unbearable. He holds my whole sex in his hand like it's a pomegranate he's testing for ripeness. The pomegranate is pulsing and about to burst open and he can sense this no doubt. He squeezes my ripeness gallantly and possessively.

We both want each other to come first. I want him inside me now more than I will after I've come, I know that, so I take control; pull him on top of me and reach down and guide him inside. He's so stiff it hurts when he pushes in, but once he starts thrusting it feels like he's started talking after all these months of muteness. A feeding frenzy follows. The sheer lightness of him after Guido Rizi is such a surprise. He comes very quickly, but he stays partly aroused and doesn't withdraw. (I knew there would be no keeping up with him this first time.)

Eventually he loses his hardness and slips out of me. In the moonlight his wet penis is still distended. He nudges me gently and turns me over onto my side so that I'm facing away from him. Lifts my hair, kisses the wet nape of my neck. With his free arm he reaches between my buttocks and his hand is squeezing the ripe splitting pomegranate again. Testing the fruit. Juicing it, kneading it, encasing the seeping pomegranate in his spread fingers until the fruit flutters and pulses and the woman in his clasp decides there's no need to restrain herself. She yells out loud for both of them.

CHAPTER EIGHT

The Morisco Boys

Today will be my final sitting for the Magdalen painting. As I wait for Enrique Rastro to join me in the shady cloister, I wonder if I will ever look upon this scene in the convento again.

The building constructions are continuing. It's been ten years since the demolition of the old Mudéjar building and it will be dozens more before the renovations are complete. Some of the gardens in the vicinity have been uprooted to accommodate a Roman fountain and pond. Two artisans come stomping across the courtyard, leaving streaks of calcined lime and clay upon the grass. In spite of these contaminations, the friars still manage to find places for secluded reading beneath the trellises and remaining trees.

A tall boy I've seen a few times before wanders past. He stops abruptly when he sees me and casually drifts back, staring at my red dress as if it's a peacock tail. 'Hello,' he says without any shyness.

I wish I could remember the child's name. What did Enrique call him? Luis? That sounds right. I saw him on the gallery with Diego Velázquez. This boy seems to feel I'm a friend not a foe. He points to a person partly obscured by the shrubbery. He's annoyed this friar has taken his own hiding-spot.

'The man will vacate the space soon,' I pacify Luis. 'He'll get up from there when they ring for the next Holy office.'

'Maybe,' Luis concedes. 'But he's still stolen my place.'

He tells me he's hoping to catch a glimpse of two new boys who arrived in the convento a week ago, but who haven't been allowed to join the others yet. He's pleased the new arrivals are Moriscos. 'Our numbers will swell from four to six!' he says and I'm very surprised. I guess he's too young to want to hide his shame.

Luis gestures, 'There they are!'

Two boys are indeed walking across the courtyard with Father Rastro. They look about ten and thirteen. Enrique has surely seen me out of the corner of his eye. But he ignores us as he enters the far cloister, returning the new Moriscos to the monks' quarters perhaps.

Enrique and Harmen were discussing the new boys during yesterday's sitting. The Moriscos are orphans of some boat tragedy. An Arab tartan capsized in rough seas off the Spanish coast. The family of deported Cordobans never made it to their destination of Tlemcen. The orphans have refused to speak since arriving in the convento. Enrique gave them a rosary and a statuette of Our Lady, and one of the boys strangled the figurine with the rosary beads. Harmen chuckled when he heard this tale.

'They weren't wearing habits, did you notice?' Luis is saying to me grumpily.

'Lucky them,' I say with a wink, eyeing his white cassock.

'I've got to find Benito,' he says and dashes off.

Father Rastro eventually joins me in the courtyard and we make our way to the round tower for the final sitting. He doesn't mention the Cordoban brothers. Upstairs, Harmen's looking forward to leaving the convento and he dances through his remaining brushstrokes. I can't stick to my pose but it doesn't matter. Harmen finished painting me weeks ago. I keep swivelling round on my knees to find Father Rastro beaming at my heels. I won't miss sitting for the painting, but I will miss this contrary priest.

The monk, whom I can always see out of my left eye, doesn't keep his pose either. He's supposed to be looking east into the future, but this afternoon he's looking at me a lot, so much so that I think I must have wiped some ash on my face. At the end of the session I get up and hug the horse round the neck and sniff his clean, musty coat and whisper in the beast's ear that I'll miss him most of all. And that's probably true.

Father Rastro waits until after we've said our farewells, and then, when he's escorting me out of the building, he broaches the matter of the Cordoban brothers.

My initial reaction is one of amusement. 'The Cordobans need a mother? Well what about me!' But yes, I quickly add, I will try my hand at mothering. If he thinks I can manage the world, how could I not succeed? (So I'll be returning, and soon!) I can't manage this deluge of bliss; I grow as stern as a nun and scowl like I've just been beaten.

Enrique is walking me down the steep stairs at the back of the round tower so we can pass by the entrance to the church. He's usually able to persuade me to step into the porch so that he can dip his hand into the basin of Holy water and sprinkle my hair in a parting blessing. 'Merciful Mary, give your daughter strength.' He appears to become another person when he enters the church. This has been his custom, but surely today will be different. I've never minded his use of the Latin (well I do a bit perhaps), but I usually find his admonitory tone hurtful. He's pinching my mind the same way that my step-mama used to pinch my upper arm to make me do the household chores. Today, though, Enrique forgets to sprinkle the water.

'They will warm to you, a woman,' he says, and something about his choice of words makes my hopeful feelings immediately deflate.

But Enrique's eyes have opened wide and he's staring at me intently, drawing himself up at the chest as if preparing to say something more important. His lips open, but then he seems to lose confidence. He takes a step backward and searches about the porch. There is a wooden table near the door and he goes over and picks up a Holy Bible. As he leafs through the gospels I'm guessing, with a sinking heart, that he's looking for the passage in Saint Luke about the woman who has a bad name, but who learnt to love Jesus after He'd absolved her huge sinner's debt.

Enrique informs me that he's going to read from Paul's twelfth letter to the Corinthians. He speaks oddly, and in fragments. 'You were baptised into Christ's body . . . we are all part of Christ . . . but each of us is a different part of his body.' He looks up at me.

I'm still preparing for that pinch.

'It is just the same with *your* body, Paula.'

And here it comes. I look down at my body as though it might hold an answer I'm supposed to give him. Yes me, a woman.

Enrique doesn't follow my gaze, but a deep-pink mark appears at the top of his cheeks.

'The parts are many but the body is one. The eye cannot say to the hand, "I do not need you", nor can the head say to the feet "I do not need you",' he reads.

I don't remember this passage in Saint Paul and I've always found parables confusing, this one no less so, with its mention of hands, eyes and feet all supposed to represent different things.

'I'll tell the Morisco boys that then,' I reply, deliberately misunderstanding. I know Enrique is saying these things with me in mind, not the boys. Anxiety darkens my perceptions and I feel that everyone is against me. In my own defence I wish I could ask him, 'And Father Rastro, are you perfect in every way?' No-one could answer 'yes' to such a question. But I'm not able to challenge Enrique Rastro because I'm in awe of him.

He seems to realise he's coarsened our moment of intimacy. He shuts the book and puts it back on the table. We walk along the ground-floor corridors, through the arches to the vestibule. I can hear the sound of my shoes and Enrique's rapping the tiles, and I hope we won't start walking in step with each other. That would be an embarrassment given that he's someone I might like to share my footsteps with in life.

When we come outside there's a melting pink and orange sunset that takes us both by surprise. It would be almost rude to ignore the spectacle, almost an insult to the nature which created it. Well, stomp on that fire and put it out too, I'm thinking, for I imagine Enrique would prefer to farewell me in more neutral surroundings. When we reach the gate I turn to Enrique and say meekly that I will see him tomorrow. Catching my curtsey of a smile, Enrique can't help himself; if I'm receptive to him he can reason with me again. As I reach out and swing the gate wide open, Enrique clutches hold of a bar to stop its swing. He clears his throat.

'Saint Paul says, if one part of the body is hurt, all parts are hurt with it. That is the thing I most wanted to tell you.'

'Oh,' I say in dismay. Enrique's blow has hit home. I avert my face and am gone without another word, wanting to make myself out of sight to him as quickly as possible. I hurry forward and fold myself into the crowd like an egg-yolk into batter, for protection, for dissolution. I save my tears until I'm far away. But I already know everything he's told me. What purpose telling a sick person they are sick?

Back in my bedchamber I go about my evening toilet and find my body has a ripe fruity odour that I've rarely smelt before, or not for many years. The smell of sex divorced from unpleasantness? I'm breathing in a musky emulsion, but who does it belong to? Memories are preserved in thoughts, but also in our senses.

Much later I visit the small garden at the side of my house to pick some peaches and pears. Afterwards I stand in the darkness listening to the crickets vibrating. Here the scent of flowers is so strong it's as though someone has pierced each of the stamens to release the perfume for my benefit.

Back inside, I drop the fruit from my apron straight onto the kitchen table. Bugs scuttle across the wood. I peel and cut a peach and share it with Violeta and Prospera. Three young women, sitting around a table, admiring the vases of each other's bodies. When Violeta goes home, Prospera yawns and drops her head in her arms. I've sewing to do, I remember. There's a new petticoat to hem. As I make my way upstairs, Father Rastro's words rebound, 'It's not just the soul, but the body too, that matters to God.' Did he really say that? And what was Saint Paul's message again? All the parts of my body are deemed of equal worth, even the part that needs the most decorating.

If I turn Father Rastro's words around, they become an acceptance rather than a judgement. Sipping orange blossom tea and drawing a needle through crisp linen, I imagine Enrique saying that he and I share the same body. He's offering his hand and eye, in exchange for my ear and foot.

That's how babies are made, isn't it. A bit of him plastered to a bit of me. But Father Rastro wants to impregnate me with the Holy Ghost, not his own emulsions. He's giving me a second chance, I suppose. I'm to be forgiven my transgressions, and not just by Enrique alone, by Our Saviour above, *venite exultemus*.

And if I am able to change, would Father Rastro do so also? Would he be into decorating my parts? That is the big question. On a day when Father Rastro played his most tutelary role with me, I refused to believe what I plainly saw. We were at cross-purposes, him wanting my weak spirit to grow in fortitude and me wanting him to honour our loving union of flesh. Some kind of alchemy was afoot, I know this for sure, because when I went up onto my balcony to find the ladder-man and take my lessons in balance, the man who caught me when I fell had lost some of his hair-pin shape. And some of the hair on the top of his head as well.

I first visit the Morisco boys two weeks after they arrive in the convento, and three days after my final sitting for the Magdalen painting.

I see them sitting listlessly in their cell, and I lose ten years. I'm as young as they are, but they don't know this yet. Telmo and Arauz greet me sourly, but at least they greet me, which is more than they do for Father Rastro. I offer the raisins I've brought, and the boys chew on the stems but they don't eat the fruit. They won't answer my friendly questions, but I've had some experience of being shunned, so I put a brave face on and begin telling them about the olive groves I tended when I was their age. I get a run-on like I do in the company of the ladder-man and, before I know it, I'm telling them about the time Hortense and I ran away to Seville and about the amazing dust-storm that happened in the terrible year of the drought.

I try to humour them as best I can. Being cooped up in a cell isn't the best place to befriend these little chaps though. If we could muck around outside I'd have a better chance, but I don't exactly have a free run of the place. Women aren't supposed to be in the convento at all, unless they're working in the kitchen. Father Rastro says yes, I can have some time alone with them as I request, but only if we stay in their cell. So here we are. Me and these Moriscos who won't give me a fair go. The older boy Telmo has turned his shoulder on me. The younger one Arauz, has closed his eyes as if he's sleepy, as if my chatter has put him to sleep. I feel a fool for opening up about myself, and don't the boys know it. But this is the way it has to be. You've got to humiliate yourself before the humiliated to make them accept you.

'Can I bring you something special next time?' Please

turn around or look up, little boys, even just once, I'm thinking. I don't want to have to tell Enrique Rastro I've failed the task.

Just as I'm leaving, Arauz gets down on his hands and knees and begins to growl. Surprised, I try to make the best of what I sense is a hostile action.

'You'd like me to bring you a dog, is that it?' I obtusely backtrack. 'I had a dog called Alanis when I was your age. I was very unhappy, you see, and he would make me laugh. He didn't understand unhappiness. I would cry and he would lick the salt from my cheeks and wag his tail at the same time. He had a black and white fluffy coat. Can you picture him? I'll see if I can bring you a doggy next time. So long, Telmo and Arauz. Keep well, won't you.'

The boys look aghast when I say these things to them, but I don't put two and two together. I'm already halfway out the door, clinging to an idea I think will make a difference to them, or at least will provide a distraction next time I call.

In the corridor I bump into Father Rastro, who must have been lurking around waiting for me to come out. I make my request but he says sorry, no dogs can be brought into the building. The next day he isn't as stern in his mettle. I could twist him round my finger. I could force the issue.

My confidence is on the rise. A week later I smuggle a silky, golden-haired spaniel into the convento. The Morisco boys and I are going to play. A little forceful persuasion never did anyone any harm. When I arrive and triumphantly reveal the dog hiding in my basket, the Moriscos draw back in disgust. I put the dog on the tiles. It squeals and cavorts about the cell.

'Dogs are dirty,' Telmo mutters between gritted teeth. 'We're not allowed to play with them.'

I suddenly remember Moors don't let dogs inside their homes. Oh, I'm so stupid. Now I'm in a quandary, with a dog to hide and time to kill. I'm going to have to change the boys' minds.

'But it is a little, indoor lap-dog and he isn't dirty. I washed him only yesterday. He cannot harm you. Tickle him and you'll see,' I plead.

Telmo and Arauz watch me patting the spaniel. They smile scornfully, as if they think I'm an idiot. They aren't interested in being converted to dog-love. The visit seems to drag on forever before I cut it short. The only fortunate thing that happens is that I'm not discovered harbouring the animal.

I'm not sure whether to bring the spaniel back, but when the next day comes round I think, oh well, I've nothing left to lose. I've had to get used to this little creature for their sake, so they can jolly well get used to it too.

The boys don't recoil in horror at the spaniel again,

but they shy away from touching it. After four visits I decide to keep the dog hidden in my basket. See if they notice or care that he's missing. Curiosity indeed gets the better of the boys. They want to know where my dog is. 'Here he is,' I say, revealing the spaniel. The dog's leaps and flurries across the tiles certainly hold the boys' attention on this day. But when the golden-haired spaniel jumps up and licks their faces, Telmo and Arauz make ugly faces, say 'yuk', and push the dog away. It starts barking, instinctively offended. I pick it up and pat it. The dog nestles close to my bosom, ceases barking and starts panting. Hopefully Father Rastro hasn't been alerted. But if he's been eavesdropping outside the door, he'll be pleased to hear what follows, as Telmo and Arauz have started chatting in Aljamiado, the Latinised version of Arabic that is their mother tongue. The boys are talking animatedly. They ask me the dog's name. I give them the choice of name, so they choose Alanis, the name of my old dog. The first sign of acceptance. When the spaniel piddles on the tiles the boys rush to help me clean it up so the priests won't find out. They've become my accomplices. We make fun of Father Rastro; we call him Father Fishface because of his limpid, watery eyes, and we mock some of the other priests that have big noses, big ears, fat lips, fat guts. And so I've changed sides, thrown my weight in with the boys, and with our combined strength we are able to pull a sunken cargo out of the sea.

'This is propitious, Paula. They have taken a liking to you,' says Enrique, a little miffed that I could do what he couldn't. Still, he grants me my due.

As I strut down the street on my way home this afternoon, my high-heeled shoes clacking like castanets, I forget to cover an eye as I usually do. Who cares if they recognise me and spit? I've healed a boy! Not one, but two. I'm either a day closer to being embraced by Enrique Rastro or a day further away from being embraced by him. When I get home I drop a copper coin in a sealed jar on my dresser. There are now one hundred and twenty coins in the jug, one for each day I've visited the Mercedarian convento. I shake the jar and jangle the coins. I shake it and I shake it and I shake it. This is money I've truly earned.

One afternoon Telmo and Arauz start talking about the disastrous boat trip. They tell me about the rickety vessel with its flimsy sail. The wild storm. The last time they saw their mother and their father. While the brothers narrate their story, they continue to pat the spaniel that is lying on its side between them, delirious from the affection it's receiving.

What he remembers most, Arauz says, was being forced into the hull with the animals. Arauz was sitting on a packing case, squeezed between his parents. There was so little room he had to sit hunched up, with his knees pressed against his chin. When the boat lurched, his knees would knock his jaw and his teeth would chatter.

'Then the water came pouring down into the hull; it was like a bath filling up, wasn't it Telmo? All the animals went swimming up on deck. Sheep and goats and mules. The animals knew what to do, didn't they Telmo? I saw you riding on the back of a giant pig.'

'I can't remember that,' Telmo replies grimly. 'When I got up on deck, I couldn't find anyone I knew. Then I saw Arauz and grabbed hold of his shirt. The boat tipped on its side and we slid straight into the sea. I didn't let go of Arauz. A sailor dragged us onto a raft. There were a lot of people in the water, holding onto luggage and animals. Some people were tipped upside-down, weren't they, Arauz?'

Arauz laughs and his body twitches. 'I thought they'd lost their money and were searching for it down below. But they were drowned.'

'Did you see any of your family again?' I have to make myself ask this question. To my relief, the boys shake their heads.

'We didn't see them in the water. We thought they would be on one of the rafts and we would meet up with them when we got back to Tarifa.'

I'm glad the boys have told me their story. I was waiting for it to happen, knowing how important it would be, like vomiting after you've suffered an attack of nausea you felt like dying for. Afterwards, the three of us stay sitting on the tiles, stroking the spaniel. 'Nice doggy,' the boys say, and 'he's a slobberer'. I have to hand it to them for being so stoical. They look pale and shocked though, as if it all happened yesterday.

When I leave their cell I sit down for a while on a bench in the Aljive courtyard. I literally can't walk any further. As it's not possible to burst into tears with the friars coming and going, I keep blowing my nose into my handkerchief. The friars look alarmed to see me sitting out here in the open. A couple of them put their hands together in prayer as they pass. I'm too upset for Telmo and Arauz to care much about my own dishonour. I already knew the facts of the boat tragedy, so why was hearing it from the boys' lips so distressing? The storytellers have carved their grief into my skin. When I was listening, all their feelings crossed over and became *my* feelings. It was *my* family who drowned and it was *I* who came so close to death.

When I recover my physical strength I get up from the bench, but I don't seek out Enrique Rastro, as is my custom. I take myself straight home. I'm grateful to Bishop Rizi that I have a secure house to go to, that I need not consider propositions from slip-sliding sailors on the street. Tonight I will be recovering upstairs and Prospera will be minding the locks downstairs. And I won't go out, not even if the ladder-man clinks his bell. I will light three candles and stare into the flames as I kneel in the dark. Maio will be purring on the rug, Alanis snuffling on the bed and I will be holding the porcelain doll that the widow in the shop that sells the miniature clothes and shoes repaired for me after I dropped it on the tiles and broke its head.

CHAPTER NINE

Paula and the Ladder-Man Go on a Pilgrimage

'How far away from Seville could we climb with our ladders?' I ask the ladder-man one evening. 'Could we move to another city?'

Earlier tonight, Bishop Rizi threw a fisherman's net over me to stop me scrambling away. With the net he pulled in a stray cat, a pine sapling and one of my shoes. I had shaken myself free, but the heel of my shoe got caught in his net. I know where my shoe fell, down the side of a building, so I will retrieve it tomorrow in the light. I'm much more nimble than I used to be. I have developed strong calf muscles and ample biceps and a few times I've been happier up the ladder than down. I suspect that I'm close to experiencing that 'balancing bliss' that skilled ladder-men speak of. Soon I'll become a true ladder-woman and be inducted into the guild. There's a candlelit ceremony that happens, apparently, and the guild leader slips over your head a ribbon from which swings a tiny copper ladder the size of a Crucifix. My ladder-man always wears his, and at the ball I saw that Hortense had a big wooden ladder hanging from a chain round her neck. When she leant over to pull up my skirt I saw it dangling in the cleft between her bosoms.

'Would it be possible to climb all the way to Cordoba?'

I still yearn for the golden city, to see the red and white arches of the Mezquita. The ladder-man smiles. He takes his slate and draws a map with houses all the way from Seville to Cordoba.

Fat chance of that being the case. 'Okay, I get it. We need buildings to climb.'

But I have excited an interest. His eyes are lively. He has something to prove. He writes with his chalk. 'Where to, Paula?'

'To the citadel of balance,' I say, for it is a place I heard ladder-men talking about at the ball. It is their Holy temple, their Mecca.

The ladder-man gestures with an extended arm. It's way too far, he indicates. He does wavy motions to show me it's over seas.

'But there's a little one, here in Seville,' I proclaim. He looks at me doubtfully. Makes his hands big then very small to show that the Seville replica is not much in comparison to the real citadel that is the size of a barrio. But yes, he assents, he will take me there if I wish.

'To our very own Sevillian citadel of balance!' I yell. (I'd stamp my foot if I hadn't lost my right shoe. I forget that shouting doesn't help the ladder-man understand. There's nothing wrong with his hearing.)

Then he draws a picture of Maio on the slate. 'We must take my cat? Why would that be?'

'You will see,' is all he will explain in chalk.

We leave the next night. We must cross the river for the pilgrimage, but we don't choose to go by boat. We go the same way as last time. Into a carriage and over the bridge and out of the carriage and up a wall. I have Maio in a pillow sack with lots of little holes punched in the fabric so he can breathe. After a while Maio stops snarling about his conveyance and I hear him purring. He's easy to please.

To the citadel of balance the three of us (plus two ladders) come. It is in cathedral quarter so we have a lot of climbing to do. It's really not easy to cross a whole city by roof and balcony. I can see why ladder-men confine themselves to a single barrio. We climb at night and during the day when the sun is burning down we sleep with members of the guild. Alongside them in their shelters. I had warned the Morisco boys, Telmo and Arauz, that I would be crossing the Mercedarian roof, and they both appeared at their dormitory window on the first night and waved to us. They had wanted to come with us, but I'd told them the journey was too far, and they wouldn't be back by morning. I feel strange and a little wicked being up here on the Mercedarian roof at night, but it's also liberating. I'm the one looking down on the priests for a change. Hee, hee! But I don't laugh for long. A bat winging past flies into the side of my head and for the rest of the night one of my ears is ringing.

In the morning we visit the shelter of guild leader Alonso who lives on top of the soap factory in San Salvador. Alonso has a sick wife and child asleep in his bed. What to do? The guild leader has a solution. We each sleep on a giant cake of soap that Alonso has dragged up through the loft from the factory floor. These cakes of soap are enormous, the size of a pallet. They're transparent, the colour of treacle or tree sap. I want to lie down, and so does the ladder-man, but I don't know what to do about Maio.

'I'll take care of Scratcher,' says Alonso, and he opens the sack and pushes Maio into an empty chicken coop.

The soap is soft and I feel more comfortable than I do when lying in bed at home. 'See, what did I tell you!' grins Alonso. 'I often sleep on the moulds before they harden.'

And much to my surprise the combined smell of black olives and orange blossom is soporific. I have no trouble falling asleep. When I get up later in the day I find that my body has left an impression of its shape in the soap. Would it be worth selling to a sculptor? I'm always on the lookout to make a few maravedís. But straight away Alonso rushes over with a mortarboard and returns the soap to its original flatness. 'Don't want it to set like that,' he says as he smoothes my effigy away.

The ladder-man's taking a good nap. We wander over to his square and understand why he hasn't surfaced yet. He's sunk so far into the mould of soap that he can't climb out. And since he's mute he couldn't tell us he was sinking. Alonso and I drag him from the hard soap he's encased in. We have to wash him down with buckets of water but even so, his eyes are running for the rest of the day. I will always go to sleep holding his hand after this, so he can squeeze me awake if he gets into strife. But I have to admit, for myself, sleeping on soap was much nicer than sleeping on cushions.

'I'm purchasing a giant cake of soap of my own,' I say to Alonso in parting, shaking his very clean hand.

'Good for you. But don't leave your soap out in the heat of the day. You've seen what can happen,' he warns, passing me a sack with a small body inside that I assume is Maio.

Our last place of rest will be the palace Alcázar. I've taken lots of walks in the palace gardens with grandée friends but I've never stepped inside the royal palace. I've pre-arranged sleepover accommodation with Harmen Weddesteeg. He's painting there on a month's assignment for the royals. He will paint three portraits: the Duke and his dog, the Duke and Duchess standing alongside the same dog, the Duke on his steed and the same dog beside them yet again. But Harmen tells me in excitement, he has already accepted a fourth commission to paint, *The Death of the Virgin*. He's going to propose me for the role of the Virgin and he wants to do a preliminary sketch when we visit, to show the Duke how I will be perfect for the part. The Duke, I suppose, might have some qualms about a woman such as me, posing as Our Lady.

The ladder-man and I have to do a lot of lever work with our ladders to get up onto the roofs of the Alcázar palace. This is our hardest act so far. Luckily Harmen is waiting for us on the highest terrace wearing a giant straw hat and squeezing orange juice to quench our thirst. We drink a gallon of juice. This man is too good to be true. Strange that he doesn't have a wife, that I know of (in Seville). And he's amused to meet my ladder-man.

'So you really exist? I thought Paula was making you up.' They smack hands together the way rivalrous men do, and Harmen sneezes and confides in a whisper, 'He smells of soap, your friend.'

The painter doesn't bother talking to my ladder-man, which hurts me a bit. If he knew the books the ladder-man read each night, he'd be impressed. But I've warned him in advance that the ladder-man can't answer back, so maybe Harmen's just being courteous.

He's received permission for us to enter through the ceiling and rest in his painting studio for the day. We climb down into a roomy attic and here I drop Maio from his sack onto the floor. He slinks around and piddles in a corner on a pile of rags. The painter doesn't seem overly concerned; he gives Maio a sardine and a piece of hard cheese. The ladder-man and I head downstairs to find a chamberpot and washtub. When we return, Maio is asleep on a rug. Harmen rubs his hands together and tells me we've no time to waste. He leads the ladder-man to a straw manger for siesta. I go behind a screen to put a black velvet costume on.

When I come out, Harmen makes me lie down on a

wooden box that looks like a coffin. He tells me to lay my hands across my chest like a statue on a sarcophagus. I have to look as if I'm dead and so it's best if I fall asleep. Then I'll look more dead than when I'm awake. I try to sleep but I stay awake. I'm too uncomfortable to fall asleep. I need a bolster under my head, but Harmen says the Virgin didn't have a bolster so I can't have one either. He pulls out his watchchain and swinging the watch back and forth before my eyes, he tries to work a sleeping trance on me. He saw this trick performed by a gypsy in Amsterdam who put to sleep a persistently vomiting child. It doesn't work on me alas, and much to Harmen's dismay, I throw up a pint of orange juice down the front of my black velvet gown. Harmen sponges the velvet vigorously and takes the Lord's name in vain. Then he pours me a goblet of brandy and tells me to drink up. I don't normally drink strong liquor so the brandy has a quick effect. I drop off to sleep with the midday sun slanting across my body.

When I wake up, Harmen has finished the sketch. I have a look over his shoulder. It really does look like I am dead. I have acquired the severe profile of the Virgin. I can see how I will look in ten years' time. I start to cry as I look at the picture. For a moment I can't work out why. Then I know. Here, before me, is my last vision of mother. She looked like this on her deathbed when she went to sleep for all time. When the ladder-man hears me crying, he wakes up and comes over to us, all flecked with straw. When he sees the drawing, he trembles and makes the Sign of the Cross. He finds it unnerving that I look so dead.

Harmen isn't dampened by our despair. He goes down on one knee and plays blind for old times' sake. 'I've lost my sight to you again, Paula.' But not his heart, I remember. It never happened; he was never even tempted. And that's how low I've sunk. To make an honourable gentleman like Harmen Weddesteeg immune to the feeling I might otherwise have engendered in him. But Harmen has always treated me respectfully. I can't really complain. And today he pays me well for sleeping the day away. It's the easiest modelling assignment I've ever had, though not without its drawbacks. I get a very sore back the next day, and in the future Harmen will admit that while I was asleep, he tied me to the crate with a rope in order to stop my constant tossing and turning. And that's when I learnt that Harmen has a sneaky, ruthless side.

I hope the Duke likes the image and I get the commission, for it's a lot easier to model asleep than awake. In parting, Harmen puts a good-luck charm around my neck. It's a little baby Jesus on a chain and it dangles precariously. The ladder-man bends over and kisses the baby as if it is a child of our love. Harmen laughs and follows suit. Then he warns me that after models play Saints they are vulnerable to the lure of dead spirits. 'Take no chances, Paula. You are possibly stranded somewhere between earth and Heaven,' he says and shakes some incense over me to ward off any evil bats or hobgoblins we might come across on our travels tonight. 'Keep telling yourself you're back with the living and you'll be okay.'

I nod. We all know about the famous model who played Saint John. Celebrating in a tavern after the final sitting, and blind drunk, he'd fallen into the fireplace and was scalded to death. The vat of burning oil in the painting had claimed him with the same searing certainty with which it had claimed Saint John.

The ladder-man and I clamber off into the night, each of us with a ladder over a shoulder and a bag of belongings tied to a wooden rung. Maio has not been forgotten. He hangs in a sack round my neck. Our final destination is one more night away. To the citadel of balance we come. Te-dum. And we meet a few returning pilgrims on the way. All ladder-men of course, and in high spirits, telling us we are in for a treat and warning us not to eat too much before we arrive. (I wonder what that's all about.)

We cross the final few buildings and the citadel comes into view, a round dome on the top of an old courthouse. We enter the portico of the dome and a citadel watchman welcomes us inside. This man is a wag. He has two cherries dangling from stems over each of his ears. Cherry earrings! He wants to know if we've brought a 'creature of balance' along with us. My ladder-man points to my bag and nods. I let Maio out and he dashes off and disappears under a curtain before I can stop him.

'You can't go in there after the cat,' the watchman warns, as I head towards the curtain. 'Not yet.'

'But I'll get Maio back, won't I?' I ask him.

'Yes, when you leave, it is possible,' he says, but he's not giving me any assurances.

'What is the purpose of the creature of balance?' I ask.

'To ensure you have understood the art.'

'Of falling into balance?'

'That's one of them,' he replies, and looks at my ladder-man knowingly.

The citadel watchman begins weighing our respective ladders. He tut tuts. 'Not a multiple of two,' he shakes his head. I can't understand what this means.

Then he wraps a ribbon around each of our ladders with a number on it and says he'll store them safely in the cloakroom with the other ladders. Off he goes, initially just with the ladder-man's property under his wing. My ladder-man looks a bit anxious but not as much as he did at the ball. He's a bit more attached to me than he is to his ladder now, I can confidently boast.

'I want to take my ladder inside with me,' I say when the watchman comes back to collect it. I've been carrying my ladder for three days. I didn't know I could get so attached to a frame of wood, but it seems I have.

'You'll be fine without it, girlie. Hold on to the señor instead. That's what he's there for.'

The ladder-man puts his arm around me, which I appreciate, but I still won't let go of my ladder. When the citadel watchman reaches for it, I hang on even tighter. Some fierce, possessive desire takes hold of me. I'm a mother about to lose a child.

The ladder-man tries to soothe me. He finds a reed pen and a square of parchment in his pocket, and writes something like this. 'The ladder can only teach you how to balance your own body. In the citadel you will learn the supreme art of shared balance.'

Reluctantly I release my ladder. I watch it all the way out of sight and out of mind, because once it's disappeared I can't believe I got so worked up over some palings of wood. I must be suffering physical exhaustion from the climb. It's very hot in here too. If I don't sit down in a minute I could very well faint.

But the citadel watchman hasn't finished with us yet. He makes both my lover and I sit in some giant scales and he tells us our individual weights. Then he hands me three stones and tells me to carry the stones in my clothing so that the ladder-man and I will be exactly the same weight. He says we will get along better if we are the same weight. I put the stones in my front pocket as I've been told. The ladder-man and I wait at the black curtain until the watchman gives us the thumbs-up to enter the citadel.

'Surely a man and a woman shouldn't be the same weight?' I whisper to my ladder-man. 'It goes against all the marriage conventions.'

The curtain thrusts in our faces and the ladder-man pulls me out of the way just in the nick of time to save me being knocked down. Two strangers are passing through the curtain on their way out of the citadel.

'Two pass out, so two can pass in,' says the citadel watchman in his singsong voice, crossing out something on his ledger. 'Two ladder-men, minus one bird.'

I look at the ladder-man for confirmation and he nods and in we go. From darkness into a spacious dome filled with lemon light. The dome is stained-glass, bringing in the sun. Rugs are being beaten. No, it's flapping wings I'm hearing, as dozens of birds whirl about our heads. At first I think that the citadel must be a giant aviary for beautiful birds. I wonder why they let my cat in here, but then I see the other animals. A monkey hanging from a pendulum is making some very indecent noises. And there are cats that must have been trained by gypsies because they're walking tightropes swung across tall balancing poles. Fluffy Persian cats with flat faces and golden eyes appear to be walking on air. Oh well, cats do have a big advantage; those rudder-like tails must help. These huge fluffy cats are hilarious. Maio will probably get into a clawing fandango with one of them. Where has that scamp of mine gone?

The sound of beating hooves comes upon us from nowhere and I clutch the ladder-man in fright. Round the edge of the floor rides a horse with some sheik-like gentleman standing on its back. 'Look at me. No hands, no reigns, no sense,' I imagine him saying. Suleiman the Magnificent apparently, and I'm waiting for him to hit the floor.

Where is Maio? I still can't see my cat. God forbid. Is that him crawling in a jiggly fashion up one of the tightropes as though he's received an invitation from the other cats? I look around to see if I'm mistaken. No, that's the only ginger cat in the citadel. The daredevil up the rope must be Maio. Spurred on by all the competition no doubt. Suddenly Maio falls in a twist but lands on his feet, then immediately starts to climb again. I shouldn't worry. Cats know their limits more than humans do. Look at the idiot on the horse!

In the centre of the floor a ladder-man is spinning a giant metal wheel around in a circle as he sits on a lever fastened to the top. He must be getting dizzy by now. Three ladder-men walk past carrying bowls on their heads. And a big man lifts another entire man on the end of a stick. What strength! I cackle in delight and the ladder-man squeezes my hand.

'It was worth the climb,' I say, 'to see all this.'

A citadel attendant, another man with two cherries slung over each of his ears, takes us by the arms and escorts us to the other side of the room. Here is the place where the pilgrim ladder-women congregate. I wave to one of the women and she signals back. I have bigger muscles in my legs now, if she cares to take a peek beneath my skirt.

'Archimedes' arms,' I say to my ladder-man, recognising the benches the couples are sitting on. The ladder-man and I are directed to one of these levers that have wooden planks as arms and a pivot point raised a metre above the floor. We copy the other couples — men and men, and also a few men with women who are already sitting on the planks working the levers. Up and down they go, on the Archimedes' arms. I sit astride an arm of our lever and the force of my weight makes the plank hit the ground with a bounce. I bite my lip and taste blood. My ladder-man knows better and slowly applies his weight to his end of our lever so that I rise back up. We begin to move up and down on the planks, testing the strength of our bearings. I realise that if I jumped off the lever I could hurt the ladder-man. He's in my power and I'm in his. And if I force myself to the ground with all my weight, as I'm doing now, I can keep the ladder-man stuck up high for ages. I enjoy doing this and the ladder-man is so tolerant he doesn't seem to mind.

He must know what I'm thinking because his expression is wry. We take care of each other; gently bouncing up and down for the most. The other couples to the left and right of us are pursuing the same motions. I suddenly feel the sonorous ease I felt as a child. My body is my own; my life in my Mama's care. A tumbler troupe came to our village one day, and I stood beside Mama and watched them contort their doughy bodies in the sun. A man did backflips through the dust. The tumblers were standing on their hands and looking at us upside-down. We children bent over and looked at the tumblers through our legs in reciprocal spirit. We giggled so much. It was a special day; but the troupe didn't come back to our village again, though I kept hoping they would.

After a while the citadel attendant comes over and balances a fat marble on the mid-point of our lever and tells us we have to try and keep the little ball still. 'If the marble rolls off, you miss out on cherries,' the attendant explains. No more jigging up and down then. The ladder-man and I have to keep the lever perfectly horizontal. And being the same weight, thanks to the stones in my pocket, this becomes possible.

Sitting on the Archimedes' arms with the ladder-man I look across at him and think that I could sit here forever and never mind. The lever is connecting our bodies. The task is collecting our minds. It is a shared purpose.

But some new pilgrims arrive and we are told our turn is over and we must get off the Archimedes' arms. 'Careful, careful,' warns the citadel attendant seeing me rise up too fast and holding me down by the shoulder so that I remain in my seat. The ladder-man and I must take care to release our weight at the same moment. When we do, and we're off the lever, the citadel attendant hands us some cherries for our ears, but I eat mine instead and the attendant shakes his finger and says 'naughty, naughty'. He gives me some more cherries to hang over my ears but I think cherry earrings look ridiculous so I eat these cherries too, but only when the man isn't looking. I put the pips in my pocket with the three stones.

Suddenly the floor begins to tip like a boat on a rough sea. I hold onto the ladder-man's arm to stop myself sliding. Someone starts yelling (not my ladder-man) but even if it's an earthquake I know I'm going to survive. I feel quite safe.

'To port, to port,' yells the attendant. 'Run that way,' he directs. And everyone is running to the left side of the citadel to make the floor straight again. It's a bit of a game. Nothing too serious. How have they managed to make the floor tip like this? We must be perched on a lever of some kind. It's a false floor, like a false ceiling. There's another beneath it probably. Now the attendant says, 'Five persons run to starboard,' for we are too many on the left side.

An attendant taps the ladder-man on the shoulder. 'Sir, your time in the citadel has expired. Others are waiting to enter.'

I don't mind leaving with the ladder-man. I feel lightheaded and serene. But then I remember.

'What about the supreme art of shared balance. I didn't get to see it.'

The ladder-man writes on his arm, 'The lever was it.'

'Oh.' But I already knew how to do that. I guess I needed reminding.

We're about to walk through the curtain when I remember Maio. There's a ginger cat like mine perched on a balancing pole at the end of the highest tightrope. 'How am I ever going to get him down from there?'

The attendant says, 'Next time, see you next time,' and pushes us through the big black billowing curtain. And I realise Maio must have been meant all along as some kind of offering or citadel sacrifice. He was always going to climb those poles and stay here with the feline lot. I'm upset with the ladder-man for deceiving me. Not such a special place after all. When we step outside the citadel I tell him I'm going to climb down from the roofs and he should come back the quick way with me to Triana in a carriage. He ums and ahs — he hates being anywhere near the ground — but finally agrees.

When we get close to the street the ladder-man starts to look sick.

'Come on. It's easy,' I cajole from the safety of the road where I stand nodding up at him.

I hail a carriage and get the driver to bring it over close to the wall, so the ladder-man can jump onto the roof, but the driver sees what my purpose is and won't let the ladder-man attempt his stunt. My ladder-man will have to put his ladder on the ground and I can see he doesn't want to do this. He's not going to do it. He starts to panic, to look around for help. Furious, I climb back up my ladder and grab hold of his leg and tell him to come down or else. He's breathing rapidly, and going red at the neck. I descend and enlist the driver for help but when I turn around the ladder-man has shifted higher up the wall again. As I watch, he scales the building in a trice and is resting his ladder against a chimney. He doesn't look back or wave goodbye as he continues his climb. I watch him get smaller and smaller then disappear between the rooftops.

The carriage driver has driven off with another paying passenger so I have to walk home to Triana carrying my ladder all the way. The midday sun is fierce. My torn gown has exposed a piece of my shoulder and it begins to burn. The other drivers are taking siesta and another carriage doesn't pass. But soon I forget my anger with the ladder-man. Maybe he knows something I don't. Of course he does. He'll turn to dust if he touches the ground, or maybe, in another life, he fell from a high tower and landed splat on his face in a pool of blood.

Usually when I come away from being with him I float free like a soap bubble. The hazy reality passes and I know who I am again. I don't have any urge to see the ladder-man until Bishop Rizi impinges, or dusk returns and the ladder-man flickers into my vision and becomes an enticing fancy.

But today I'm missing him on solid earth. I clutch the three round stones in my pocket that make our weights match. I keep looking round for him and seeing people who I think are him. I know when I see him again I shall tell him that I've learnt the art of shared balance. And I'll thank him for that.

CHAPTER TEN

Diego Velázquez Takes Another Stroll About the Town

Mid-summer and Seville is whitewashed and North African. Few sleep during siesta and many don't retire at all. Like me, they prefer to sit in their patios fanning themselves, dipping bare feet into water-pails drawn from the deepest, coolest wells. I'm sitting in the plant-filled patio, doing exactly this when my master Pacheco approaches from the lane, rolls down a stocking and shares a pail with me.

The afternoon heat is bonfire strong. The water gurgling in the miniature fountain is providing a phantom coolness. Pacheco's fifteen-year-old daughter Juana can't sleep either. She enters the patio, swaddled in white linen like a newborn babe. She serves us dates so moist they melt in my mouth. I feel like I'm about to melt too. Keeping still is sometimes worse than moving about. Yet when I was moving around earlier, I decided the opposite was true. Juana hands me a glass of apricot nectar, then disappears, but through the doorway I catch a glimpse of her unwrapping the linen cloth from her head and body. She's unwinding her clothes like a bandage. Poor thing. To have to dress up like that to come outside. But the patio is open to the street and Juana is almost a woman now.

It's weeks since I visited the Mercedarian convento and witnessed the painting of the penitent woman. When I came home that day, I decided to tell Pacheco where I'd been and what I'd seen. Rather than admonishing me, he congratulated me on my initiative. (Lucky it didn't go the other way.) He informed Carlos Zamorana that Paula Sánchez was sitting for a painting which featured Father Rastro, and that, more importantly, Castle inspectors had been invited to view the painting. Zamorana's inquiries into misconduct were temporarily suspended, pending the result of the Castle visit. The monk did not lie, because the inspectors visited the Mercedarian convento the day after I did. The painting was not condemned, but it was judged to be an indecent work of art. The commissioner and future owner of the painting, Doña Fillide, would be required to keep it in a private room and not display it before a public audience of any kind.

Pacheco and Zamorana learnt pretty quickly of the outcome of the Castle inspection. This wasn't surprising as both are part of the Inquisition's censorial network of communications that extends across Europe and even as far as the New World. There's a bit of a distinction though. The government-appointed Castle Inquisitors have munitions and guards at their disposal, they are a centralised force appointed by Royal Charter in Castile, whereas Zamorana and Pacheco are inspectors who answer to His Holiness the Pope, in Rome.

My master had several further discussions with Carlos Zamorana about the painting. He confided in me that Zamorana had developed an obsessive interest in the work of art and had requested an independent viewing, but Father Rastro has refused to let Zamorana into the convento for this purpose. Good on him, I thought. Rastro is wise to keep the harshest (if also the most intellectual) of Sevillian inquisitors away.

Pacheco trusted me enough to accept my opinion of the painting without seeing it for himself. He was curious about it though, in his circumspect fashion, and would no doubt find a way of viewing it in the near future.

As we sip the unpleasantly furry juice and soak our feet,

Pacheco says to me, as if reading my mind:

'The Weddesteeg painting is dry now, or so I hear. It will soon be delivered to Fillide Rosano. '

'You'll get to see it for yourself at her party then,' I say, cheekily.

Pacheco smiles. 'Doña Fillide won't wish to break Castle regulations. But I may get the privilege of a private viewing, I suppose . . .'

With our feet sharing the bucket of water, it seemed the most fortuitous moment to broach another matter with him.

'The Morisco boy, Luis — remember Luisito? He's seeking release from the Mercedarians.'

'Ah, the boy of your marvellous drawings!' Pacheco over-enthuses, as though to cover up his real feelings.

'I think I could persuade my family to take him in,' I say, the idea having just occurred to me. 'They have need of an extra hand.'

'Father Rastro won't want to set a precedent by releasing one of his Morisco charges,' Pacheco replies matter-of-factly.

'But you could possibly ask?' I need to tell Luis I at least *tried* to help him.

'You know, Diego, Luis will be free to come and go in a few years' time. He will be a respected member of our community if he plays his cards right, and the fuller his commitment to the Catholic faith, the better. Quite a privilege to be one of the few remaining Moriscos . . .'

I withdraw my sympathy when Pacheco says, 'You know, Diego . . .' I have some purchases to make for my master in town, so I use this as an excuse to head off on my own. It's still uncomfortably hot, but I want to get away. It crosses my mind that I might run into Catarina taking a post-siesta stroll in the company of a duenna, or perhaps with one of her sisters.

I exit through the stable into the laneway behind the house. I don't yet know which way I'm going to walk, but my legs, like a horse's, guide me along a much-frequented route. Before long I'm in the open-air market of San Lorenzo, passing along a garish thoroughfare, breathing in dust of cinnamon and cloves. A spectacle of glazed fruits is attracting both flies and children. I keep walking, but round the next corner I slow for a moment to brush my hand against a red and gold hanging tapestry, to price a sapphire-blue Aegean bowl.

As the afternoon shadows lengthen, more stalls open. The bazaars fill with shoppers and I hear foreigners speaking many tongues: Castilian, Berber, Arabic, Persian, vulgar Italian, French, Catalan, and even some English. Before I forget what I came here to do, I make my purchases for Pacheco. It's easy to get sidetracked. Rare produce from the

New World is attracting a flurry of onlookers. Small exotic creatures tremble inside wooden crates. I stop to watch a tailor measuring a furry raccoon for a length of lapel. Turn down the next aisle and I'm greeted by a tumult of chirping birds. A milliner has his arm thrust inside a cage and is counting plumes on a green and yellow parrot. I imagine him festooning hat after hat after hat.

As I continue walking the stalls peter out, replaced by residential properties. Wrought-iron gates reveal chequered patios and shady courtyards where people are sitting, standing, squatting, sweeping the rush matting and drinking wine and syrups. The houses are mainly whitewashed but their fences are made from mud and sand and the colours blend where they join. High walls are engulfed by jasmine and jungle-bursts of creeper. I love the huge pink fluted flowers that hang upside-down and trail pollen across the cobblestones.

I get a heady mix of fear and entitlement walking the streets. I might be attacked by *pícaros*, but I can run fast if I have to. Around each corner is another familiar face, a friend maybe. I raise my hat to the Duque de Medina. And here is one of Pacheco's servants lugging a sack of groceries. I nod to the servant who's limping with his load, and he curses me. I should help him out, I know, but he's going the opposite way.

Whether those who pass are high or low in rank, I always nod politely, but I like to keep on walking so as not to upset the flow of images, the sense of an unending river of people coursing by, and me as part of this river. I watch the faces moving into focus from a distance — some eyes look at me, some look away. I see all at once, the veiled or candid expressions, the colour of tiles in the patios, the spurt of water, the curving rays of daylight, the blackbirds beaking the fruit, the peel in gutters, the fragility of infants. A litter bearing a dead child, carried by weeping mourners, is the only thing I can't look directly at this afternoon; instead I find myself pretending to remove an obstruction from the corner of my eye.

A little later, I'm overtaken by a religious procession for Saint Stephen of Hungary, an odd saint who demands that all his subjects marry. Pushing through the chanting crowd, I take refuge in an inn and wait for the procession to pass, peering through a small window whose panes are made of oiled parchment. The bartender keeps looking at me suspiciously, so I buy a pint of ale and give it away. (I'm not supposed to drink alcohol.) When the noise of fifes and drums has faded, I emerge from the bar, changing course to avoid running into the procession again. Turning down a laneway I've never noticed before, I hesitate in front of a Carmelite convento which advertises itself with a commemorative plaque. Inside the gate is a stark patio lacking the usual Arabic tiles and refinements. Waxed gardenias in the window boxes are the only vegetation in sight. It is a small establishment, as are all female religious orders. I look at the first-floor windows with their drawn blinds. What time does siesta end in this place? Perhaps the blinds are drawn to stop novices looking out. I remember that I've come on this stroll hoping to find Catarina. Perhaps she's destined for the cloister? For a moment I picture the slightly fabulous Catarina of the carnival (with her dusty skirt and conniving plans) enveloped in a black habit. Then I think better of it.

A fat old nun enters the patio. It looks like she's coming to check on me, and judging by her square jaw she means business so I hurry back to the main streets and into the crowded thoroughfares. As I try to regain the jubilant rhythm of my former footsteps, I'm thinking of Luis again. How can I help the young Morisco if Pacheco won't take an interest in him? Luis's life-story is never going to be of his own making. His footsteps aren't going to tap time with history as mine have been doing this afternoon, navigating the uneven flagstones of Seville, treading the streets almost proprietarily, at liberty to savour the call of vendors, the rustle of girls' starched skirts, the tinkle of the tambourine drifting across the wide-angled squares. It is to

be my privilege, rather than Luis's, to monitor the temper
and climate of the day, to watch the residents moving
fast and slow about their tasks, to fear those who press
too closely, to regret the groans of the cripples from the
church porches, the blind with their outstretched hands,
the lame soldiers hobbling past in military garb always with
a limping melody about their footfall. It is to be my fate,
not Luis's, to search the faces of the unlucky till my eyes
are sore, until the things I don't want to see eventually
turn me back to the safer, freshly washed laneways and the
plump-faced infants borne by lemon-scented women in
my home barrio, San Vicente.

I sit down on an empty, unshaded bench away from
the other people in the square. I find a reed pen and my
pocketbook and begin drawing illustrations. I can't rid my
mind of the earlier conversation with Pacheco. It's out of
our hands, Pacheco was implying. Luis should have been
born a couple of centuries earlier, or in another place.

I've read what the broadsheets have to say on the issue.
The Inquisition wants these Morisco children to stay in
Spain rather than follow their families across the ocean.
At seven years of age the children are no longer bound
by the prohibition keeping them in Christian lands. Many
exiled parents are waiting to be reunited with their forsaken
children. Some have sent Berber merchants with ransom

money, but the Church is reluctant to let their charges go. They feel obliged to protect the youngsters, and there are hundreds of them, from the curse of Islam.

I find myself sketching the bell at the friary gate. I picture Luis walking out the gate with a big smile on his face, his departure officially sanctioned. I make a few more silly doodles, then for no obvious reason I find myself sketching the Weddesteeg painting, the two foreground figures and the vertical post of the Cross that splits the painting down the middle. In the painting, as I remember, Paula has pride of place at the centre, kneeling directly in front of the Cross. This is a clue for some reason, and when I get up from the bench I don't go back to Pacheco's or continue my search for Catarina. I begin walking south, my sights set on the houses of Triana that soon come into view on the other side of the river.

I've never visited Paula, of course, but I've a rough idea where she lives, and perhaps a neighbour will be able to point out her street. I've no intention of calling on her. I just want to see where she lives. If I run into her coming across the bridge that will be a blessing.

Triana smells like a potter's workshop. Here they make ceramics in abundance. Fumes are resinous and earthy and make me lustful. I lose myself in unfamiliar streets. I can't bring myself to ask anyone where she lives. Eventually I stoop down and ask a couple of children who won't think the worse of me if they know who she is. They look a bit puzzled but they point out a street and I thank them. I turn down the next calle instead, so it comes as quite a shock to see Paula's maid scrubbing a doorstep on my left. I increase my pace but my shoe strikes a stone. Too late, the maid has risen from the step, has recognised me, is calling out my name and urging me back. (How does she know me? But of course, she's overheard my conversations with Paula in the marketplace.) I reluctantly make my way up to the door. The maid informs me that Paula is at home. I wait in the patio, dreading the meeting. What if I've called at an inconvenient time? Imagine if Paula is entertaining Bishop Rizi upstairs right now? To calm my nerves, I peruse the ceramic wall tiles. Most are decorative, but some have interesting pictures painted on them. A naval vessel, the *Santa María*, one of Columbus's ships, catches my eye. And a pretty moss-brown rabbit, captured in flight.

A short time later Paula appears, wearing a mud-green dress and carrying her toy dog. She even looks great in green. You couldn't say the same about most women.

So there will be no misunderstanding about the reason for my visit, I quickly come to the point. Can she talk to Father Rastro? Make him see how unfortunate Luis's situation really is?

Paula walks over to me and transfers the spaniel into my arms. 'I can take this little doggy into the Mercedarian fort when I'm not supposed to, but I'll be damned if I can carry a boy out in his place! You're asking too much of me.'

I clutch the squirming dog.

Paula bends her head to turn back the cuff on the sleeve of her gown. When she's folded it in place she looks at me again.

'Many of the boys were never meant to be in the convento,' she agrees. 'They each deserve a better future, and a different past as well.'

She smiles accommodatingly. 'What would you like to drink? Chocolate? Coffee? Wine?' She's ringing for her maid.

I've turned my back on Paula so I can stroke the spaniel without her watching me. I don't usually drink these substances. Chocolate is too sweet, coffee too bitter, and I have yet to acquire a liking for wine. Hasn't she got any orange juice?

'The Moriscos are better off with the Fathers than with the brutal minders in the orphanage,' Paula continues.

She would know about such things, I suppose. But I persist.

'Luis thinks his mother and sister have settled in Morocco. He would like to join them, or try and bring them home.'

The maid appears at the door. Paula quickly takes her dog back from me. Now I have nothing to protect me but my belief in Luis's cause and my trust in Paula Sánchez.

'It is such a surprising thing, Paula! And yet it is not so surprising,' I burst out. 'The Mercedarians, an order founded to ransom Christian slaves in Muslim lands, are getting their own back. By imprisoning Moriscos they are evening up the score, aren't they? Some of the Fathers spent years in Algerian prisons. They are still holding the pirate infidel to account.'

Paula is silent.

'Yes, Diego, but these boys were *born* here,' she eventually replies in her soft, reedy voice. 'They speak our language perfectly. They are like our own, and we would not wish to see our own . . . *hurt*.'

Father Rastro must have been influencing her.

'I'm already helping Telmo and Arauz,' she explains.

She must be able to sense my disappointment because she gives in pretty quickly.

'Perhaps you're right about securing Luis's release,' she nods. 'I'll talk to Father Rastro. He may not be averse to your proposal. But no more talk of this matter now. What will you drink? Are you listening, Violeta?'

CHAPTER ELEVEN

Paula Learns Some Aljamiado in the Mercedarian Convento

The Cordoban brothers have moved into the dormitory with the other Moriscos so we meet in the Major courtyard and I join them at their games of bat and ball. When I'm in their company I lose ten years, become girlish again. I suspect that's why the boys like me, because I'm more of a sister to them than the surrogate mother I'm supposed to be. I don't take the spaniel into the convento any more. He can't be conveniently hidden when we're playing out of doors. That leaves me to be the playful one.

If I have any maternal feelings to speak of, they're blossoming for Enrique Rastro. But the maternal is, in this case, born of the womanly. When I'm in his company I expand like a water lily. My petals open out. It's love, I suspect, but not always pleasurable. Sometimes I want to run away out of sheer awkwardness: the self-hatred rising in my chest. I'm uncertain how to proceed, whether Enrique wants to move things forward, or would be happy continuing in this impulsive yet essentially repressed fashion. My greatest fear is of having my special privileges (in the convento) withdrawn and of further loss of face.

This morning I got up early to bake a walnut cake for Enrique. While I was beating the eggs and sifting the flour I was dreaming of those afternoon sittings for the Magdalen painting. My favourite memory is of Enrique helping me up off the floor.

I made up a song to go with egg beating and walnut crushing. 'Touch me, he touches me not,' I began humming, 'He touches my arm, but his eyes say, "touch me not". He helps me up, but his eyes say, "don't touch!" *Noli me tangere.* He touches me, he touches me not. He loves me, he loves me not.'

Today Father Rastro greets me in the cloister and looks questioningly at my basket. Perhaps he can smell the buttery aroma. Suddenly it seems too forward to reach in and give him the cake as I'd intended; I shall keep it for the boys instead.

'How are the Cordobans?' I ask.

Enrique is frank for a change. He's concerned that the brothers, especially Telmo, are dominating the other boys. The Moriscos have begun taking their ablutions very seriously. On Fridays they usually bathe in a terracotta tub in an alcove adjacent to the Major courtyard. What has aroused Enrique's unease is the quietness and privacy they command while bathing.

It is Friday today and Enrique and I are standing in the cloisterwings, watching the boys ferry water from the fountain to the tub. The six boys then squeeze into their circular bath and begin mopping themselves with sponges.

'They're as ordered as they are in Mass,' Enrique reflects softly, almost to himself. We move closer to the alcove, but remain concealed behind a roman pillar.

'Let's bless our faces first,' I hear Telmo encourage Remi as he sponges the little boy's mouth for him. The Moriscos are praying to each part of their body, conducting an Islamic ablution ritual.

Father Rastro looks perplexed when he hears these profanities. He ventures out into the open, moves into the boys' sanctuary, and is sprayed with water. Soaked in fact.

'Peeping Tom!' Telmo shouts, as though Father Rastro has come to leer at their circumcised penises. Rastro stops in his tracks like a cornered animal.

Little Arauz jumps up in delight, exposing his slippery nakedness, and squeals, 'He's a peeping Tom!' pointing at the priest accusingly.

I stifle a laugh with my hand. A soaked Enrique hurries away to change his outfit. These boys sure know how to keep the priests at bay. Thankfully they haven't seen me yet. I'm not exactly hiding from them, but I keep myself out of view.

After washing away their sins, they wrap themselves in towels and slump down on the tiles to honour Allah. Six naked boys, arms outstretched, pointing in the direction of Mecca. Father Rastro would be further incensed to see this, but to me it seems harmless enough.

'God there is no god but He, the Living, the Everlasting,' Telmo recites as he kneels on his towel, now being used as a prayer mat.

The boy I'm fondest of is Arauz. I watch him with a smile. His towel is a magic carpet, perhaps, and in his mind he's flying across the Strait of Gibraltar to Tunis and the spireless African towns where no bells ring, and further afield, across the yellow sands to Mecca itself. I wonder if the boys are really facing Mecca in their prayers. Actually, if I have my bearings right, I think they're pointing towards Rome.

Father Rastro returns to the alcove in dry attire,

unperturbed. The boys are on the alert and prayer mats quickly became towels again. They have invented what they call 'the dance of the towels' to put Enrique off the scent.

'The dance of the towels?' inquires Enrique of the boys, as the naked Moriscos flutter their towels to the right and to the left of him.

'Was invented by the Romans to keep warm, after bathing, in mid-winter,' Telmo puffs, as he runs around Father Rastro, flapping his damp towel towards him provocatively then wresting it away.

The Moriscos have lost all their former modesty it would seem.

'Tell us about your brother in Algiers,' Luis pleads, as Enrique begins to supervise their dressing. I know that Enrique has a brother called Felipe who writes to him regularly from his *bagnio*, an Ottoman prison-house for Christians who've been put up for ransom.

'My brother writes that he enjoys his afternoon stroll in the prison garden,' replies Father Enrique mildly, obviously touched that the boys remember his brother.

'And what of his clothing?' the boys ask excitedly. I get the idea they know the answer.

'It is Moorish.'

This fact makes the boys smirk.

'And what of his diet?'

Enrique Rastro glances at me hiding behind the pillar, then turns back to the boys. 'It is herbs and tough figs.'

The boys shake their heads in amusement and disbelief.

'And what of his ransom?'

'It is still too high.'

'Still too high to pay?'

The boys convey amazement, yet they must have known this would be Father Rastro's answer. They mock and pity his forsaken brother.

Shortly afterwards, Telmo and Arauz notice my presence and come dashing over to say hello. When I reveal the contents of my basket, the other boys converge on me and attack the cake like ravenous dogs. Father Rastro says he must return to the administrative wing and he delegates us another minder. It's the monk who features in the painting *The Penitent Woman*. Father Rastro addresses him as Victor María, and I take note of his name this time. He escorts us around the back of the building to a dusty square where the choirboys (and some of the young priests) regularly play handball.

'Two at a time on the handball court,' Victor María advises. He will act as umpire. 'One, three,' 'One, four,' I hear him calling out the score. Scuffling feet stir up the dust. Arauz holds my hand as we watch Remi and Benito tear about the court. Arauz tells me he has a sore neck and he will not play today.

'How long has your neck been hurting?' I ask him.

'All my life.'

'All your life?' I say in disbelief.

'Well, for as long as I can remember.'

'His pillow is too fat,' says his brother knowingly.

'It's not because my pillow is too fat,' Arauz sulks.

Telmo picks up a tennis bat and gives me another and we have a less competitive game of our own at the side of the handball court. Telmo forgets where he is and whacks the ball over my head and up onto a roof. 'Oh no!' He and Arauz run to get a ladder. When they return Victor María sees what they're up to and comes off the court to help out.

'It's your turn, Telmo,' he says, directing the bigger boy over to the court.

I hold the ladder and Victor María climbs up onto the roof and shifts precariously along the uneven tiles, searching in the gutters for the ball. Arauz and I watch in concern. Victor María ducks down for a moment, then the missing ball flies over our heads. Arauz gives chase.

'No more tennis,' I say, when Arauz returns, bouncing the ball up and down. I collect the ball and the bats and put them in a string bag slung over my shoulder.

While we watch Telmo and Luis spinning around on the dirt court the weather changes and dark clouds blot out the midday sun. We hear thunder, and shortly afterwards rain pours down in a deluge. Victor María herds us to the nearest shelter and pushes open the door. It's a music room that joins onto the back of a stage. This must be where the musical priests keep their instruments. Before the monk or I can stop them, the boys are plucking lutes, strumming guitars and blowing through the holes on flutes.

Victor María warns, 'Be gentle with those instruments.' But he doesn't seem to have the conviction to tell them to stop. They're not doing any harm. They have grubby fingers but it hardly matters. How they love pretending they can play music.

I cease worrying about them. Stand at the open door staring at the marble curtain of rain. The convento outside and its walls have disappeared from sight. The rain is wetting the floor at my feet. Victor María comes over and stands behind me. We stare at the downpour together. The rain is so dense it looks like a flock of seagulls. Victor María asks me to stand back away from the rain. 'The instruments might get wet,' he softly explains, closing the door. He brings me a chair. Arauz sits at my feet and dries his wet hair on my velvet skirt. And I let him.

We watch Telmo jangling finger cymbals and

shimmying his hips. 'Boys, we are Moros, not Moriscos, and we dance the *zambra*,' Telmo sings. He's teaching the others the movements of the rhythmic dance he and his relatives must have enjoyed in their private patios. Again Victor María does nothing; perhaps he has no authority here. Luis, the boy Diego Velázquez is so keen to help, is shaking a tambourine for all its worth. The volume of noise inside the room drowns out the chorus of rain.

Telmo is speaking the boys' mother tongue, Aljamiado. 'If we don't speak it, we'll forget it,' he says, and he insists the boys call themselves by their Muslim names: Ali (Telmo), Abdullah (Arauz), Harun (Luis), Abu (Remi) and Hasan (Camilo). Names they were given at birth. The others they acquired at Catholic Baptism in our churches, a week later.

'I can't remember my inside name,' says Benito to the name-reciting boys.

'You must have one — everybody does,' insists Telmo.

'But I can't remember what it was. I've been here since I was three.'

Benito starts to cry.

'Paula could find out from Father Rastro. It'll be on your documents,' Telmo says.

'Father Rastro won't tell her,' declares Luis.

'Yes he will. He's sweet on her, plain as the nose on his face,' insists Telmo.

The boys look at me questioningly. Half of me is thrilled that they think Father Rastro likes me (well, they'd know, wouldn't they?), and the other half of me feels exposed.

Victor María steps forward. 'You can have my inside name Benito. Because I don't use it. You can be "Muhammad", for the dance.'

The monk is a convert? Funny how you don't notice someone's dark skin until you're looking for it. But yes, he does look a bit Arabic come to think of it.

Benito is furrowing his brow. 'Muhammad?'

'Doesn't it sound like you?' Luis asks.

'It sounds like other boys,' Benito complains.

Telmo distracts Benito by giving him some personal instruction on how to achieve the soft, fluid movements of the *zambra*, and soon the two of them are oscillating their torsos to the guitar's vigorous, if untuned thrum. I can't help but be impressed. (The ladder-man is the only man I know who would be able to jiggle his midriff in such an agile way.)

A little later the rain stops. Victor María checks outside to see if we can return to the handball court. He comes inside quickly, securing the door carefully.

'Father's out there,' he says, looking embarrassed.

'Who is?' I ask, too loudly, standing up and smoothing down my skirt.

'Father Rastro. He's waiting to come in,' Victor María hushes me.

The boys, alerted to the proximity of their Mercedarian leader, switch from the Moorish *zambra* to the Spanish chaconne just in case. Not much of a change, as it happens, for these dances share the same percussive footsteps.

But Father Rastro doesn't come inside. Luis wanders over to the closed door and stands with his ear pressed against the wood. 'I can hear someone,' he whispers. Luis knocks softly on the door from the inside. No answer. Luis knocks again, more loudly this time. He's knocking the wrong way around, but he feels the need to acknowledge Father Rastro's presence perhaps.

And then it happens. A puzzled Rastro opens the door.

'Yes, Luis?'

'You were waiting outside the door, Father,' Luis comments.

'Yes, I was.'

Father Rastro must be expecting Luis to invite him inside now. But Luis understands what Father Rastro is really here to do, which is to eavesdrop on us. He smiles at Father Rastro in a friendly, accepting way then closes the door on him. We're all standing around stunned. I hesitate, then rush to the door to open it for Enrique, but he has already taken his leave of us and is walking away. My voice catches in my throat. I'm unable to call him back.

I intended broaching the subject of Luis's release with Enrique Rastro today, but I don't see him after the door-knocking incident. When I enter the Mercedarian offices the following Monday, I'm informed that Father Rastro is no longer in Seville. Apparently he's gone to Castile for at least six weeks. 'Regretfully,' the official adds, 'you will no longer be needed in the convento.'

'I am not to come again?' I can't believe it.

Enrique must have turned against me. Something I've done or said has offended him. Perhaps he's tired of my beauty, or has found it frustrating to look upon that which he can never embrace. Or worse still, he's realised that my nature is dull, my lack of education appalling, my crooked teeth a sorry sight. He has finally seen the truth, that I'm a worthless, fallen woman of no value to a learned Holy man. Of course I don't belong in the friary. As an artist's model I could pass inside, but only through sheer luck. How could Enrique have ever thought I could come in here and not remain a secret? I wore thin my welcome when I began to be seen regularly out of doors.

Who can I confide my anguish in? On my way home I decide to visit Harmen Weddesteeg and to this purpose I cross the city and enter the forecourt of the Alcázar palace. Here I'm told Harmen isn't in residence this day, and as I don't know where else to look for him, I return to Triana, crossing the bridge at a child's pace. 'And I thought Enrique was such a good person he would never hurt me.'

Once home, I avoid my servants and go straight upstairs to cuddle my lap-dog, Alanis. It's a shame, I think, as the dog licks away my salty tears, but worse has happened, much worse. I can cope with this loss.

I've avoided seeing Bishop Rizi for a whole month. It wasn't Father Rastro's subtle recommendations but his habitual presence at my side that have fortified my resolve. I've been living for the furtive, elated moments I got to spend with Enrique in the convento.

In bed with Guido Rizi later the same day, I close my eyes and imagine it's Enrique who is fondling my breasts and stroking my thighs. I muffle a squeal when Guido's fingernails intrude in my most sensitive parts. That didn't happen. Enrique would handle me like fine paper; he would never do such a thing. While Guido transports himself on top of me, I grind my teeth and silently cry out to Enrique for help.

CHAPTER TWELVE

Paula Learns the Ladder-Man's Big Secret

My sojourns with the ladder-man had been keeping pace with my visits to the convento until Enrique Rastro left for Castile. What the Mercedarian leader inspired in me, the ladder-man fulfilled. Once, during lovemaking, I even called the ladder-man Enrique by mistake. The ladder-man wrote on his slate, 'Who's Enrique, for God's sake?'

'Tell me *your* name first,' I demanded.

'If I tell you, will you promise never to mention it to anyone, or start calling me by that name?' he wrote.

I promised of course.

'AURELIO,' he wrote in big letters.

'Aurelio,' I whispered, and showed my gratitude by fulfilling his desires late into the night.

But yesterday, the day after Father Rastro left Seville, Aurelio had a fall on the roof and cracked his ladder in two places. Today he's retiring under his shelter like a man with a broken leg. I tell him I'll take his ladder down to the place of streets and horses and have it repaired. He writes that the wood is split and it's irreparable, but I insist. Modern carpentry can work wonders. I'll leave him my own beautiful amber ladder instead. When I carry his ladder away he sheds a little tear. He may not see it again. But, if worse comes to worse, it will do him good to have a new ladder.

I visit six carpenters who all say it cannot be fixed before I find one who agrees to repair it. 'It'll cost more than a new one though.' That is okay, I say.

He has a little workshop in the main street of town, with lots of folding doors. I can't find my way into the shop and, then, when it's time to go (having secured the deal) I can't find my way out. When I return to collect the ladder the next week, the carpenter says something that surprises me.

'I made this ladder, five years ago.'

'You did?'

He shows me some hieroglyphic indentations on the side beam. Then, as if to impress me, he goes over to a desk and consults a heavy ledger. I watch him running his finger up and down the margins till he finds the reference he's seeking.

'Ah, it's Aurelio's ladder.'

I stare open-mouthed.

'Still up on the rooftops, is he?'

I'm sworn to secrecy.

'He may have changed his name,' I reply, wriggling out of committing myself to knowing him.

The carpenter is persistent, 'The mute lad. Minus a tongue?'

I pause for a few seconds. How stupid I was not to realise.

'What happened to his tongue?'

'Didn't you know? Zamorana culled it.'

I don't have to pretend to look appalled. 'What was the crime?'

The carpenter snickers. 'Bit of back passage stuff, or so I heard. Jilted lover he did it to betrayed him.'

'A female lover?'

'Of course,' he says indignantly. 'What are you thinking, lass? He'd have lost his head if he'd done it with a man.'

I go home carrying Aurelio's ladder under my arm, trying not to swing it about and knock people down. I'm feeling so dejected that a couple of men say to me in passing, 'It's not that bad, is it Missy?'

My poor little ladder-man. Thousands do it, and he had to be the one to get caught. And what sort of woman would have betrayed him on a matter so intimate? He doesn't choose his women well. That's a worry because of what it implies about me.

The sky is purple tonight. An oyster moon hovers, silky and generous, though not as full as yesterday. Aurelio and I exchange ladders and blank kisses in the dusk. There's a fish for him to eat that Prospera baked at my request. As he eats, I watch him like a hawk, but there's no seeing into his mouth. We can't ever talk to each other and we can't kiss properly either, but we can do all that really matters with our bodies in the dark.

CHAPTER THIRTEEN

In the Casa de Rosano with Diego Velázquez

They are only hands. I'm somewhat relieved. A pair of small, soft hands are forcing my eyelids closed. Warm breath at the back of my neck, and muffled chatter. Beneath the enfolding hands, a slit of light. The lacy hems of women's gowns and dozens of slippers, scampering.

I was sitting innocently by the pond staring at the stagnant goldfish when someone attacked me from behind. I decided not to resist. The hands were delicate and scented. The high-pitched laughter clearly female. Those fancy satin slippers told me a party ruse was underway.

Shortly before the incident, I'd arrived at the widow

Rosano's mansion with Pacheco. I took one look at the glittering guests and searched for the nearest exit into the garden. My clothes weren't formal enough and I didn't have a bejewelled mask to match those that some of the guests were wearing. If I'd had one of those masks to put on, as a disguise, I would have followed my master into the crowded hall.

The secluded courtyard seemed a safer option. But the slippered fiends had snuck up on me as I sat at the edge of the pond, staring at the bloated goldfish. A hissing fountain and ribald frogs assisted the girls in taking me unawares.

Now mischievous hands are slipping a blindfold over my eyes. The fastening fingers are clumsy and a piece of my hair catches in the knot. Many hands are patting my arms, tugging on me, making me stand, twirling me around so that I go with them, dizzily. I let myself be led away. (If they've managed to steal my purse they'll be disappointed; it's virtually empty.)

I'm guided away from the indoor music. For a moment, a small clammy hand, holding my own. Then the animal moan of a gate opening and closing. We have entered a more ample garden. The scent of plants is strong and I feel solid earth underfoot. I'm led hastily, so that I can't help but stumble and trip. I fall forward, knocking someone down. A girl whimpers in pain. Angered, I want to rip off the blindfold and smack them all. I'm on my own with these scurrilous nymphs. The scuffling slippers come to a halt. The hands make me sit down on a hard bench. Muffled directions are given. Scented bodies press close and excitement tames my annoyance. A sharp stone or ring grazes my chin. I grab at air. Nothing. A shaking sound over my head. Something soft; feathers falling? Whatever it is tickles as it slides down the back of my neck, inside my shirt. Ouch! A wire obstruction has been placed on top of my head. It doesn't hurt for long, but later I can't work out why I didn't force the blindfold off at this point. Say enough is enough.

Instead I continue to sit, disarmed, compliant.

The chorus of girls is laughing and then multiple slippers are running away. Am I abandoned? The footsteps peter out. I hear a gate in the distance squeak open and clang shut. I've been left on my own, apparently. A lizard or bird shifts in nearby leaves. I'm still unsure if I should pull off the blindfold. Isn't something else going to happen? I remove the wire contraption from my head. Loosen the blindfold. In the moonlight I find myself covered in leaves and petals. The wire coronet in my hand is a garland. Flowers are piled high on the ground at my feet. I stand up and wipe the decorative coating from my clothes, empty my pockets of petals and leaves, shake myself tidy as best I can. But a lot of the petals stick to me.

So this is what girls do, do they?

I go back to the noisy hall, no longer shy. Then I see
Catarina. Masked, like the first time I saw her. Encircled
by her sisters, each a shorter version of herself. The four
sisters coalesce under party lamps, age-weighted from tall
to small as gritty gold, amber, hazelnut, and the youngest
whom I liken to boiled toffee. Shining with success,
gossiping and giving cheek. I can't prove it, but I know it
was them, for sure.

I haven't stopped missing my goldfinch. Every time
I pass Catarina's house in San Pedro I listen for its song.
I look through the gate into the patio hoping to see my
cage hanging from a tree. Maybe I'll see a flutter of wings
dipped in yellow. How I'd smile to see your spry head jut
once again, goldfinch. Actually, I wouldn't mind if this girl
Catarina is the thief. What I love, she perhaps chooses to
make her own.

Once I saw a nun emerge from the Loyola gate with
Catarina's mother in tow. Two old women, but no sign of
a seductive daughter. I crossed the road and bought some
water from the vendor who's always working there. As I was
drinking I stole a clandestine look back at the house. The
curtains had opened upstairs and four sisters stood bunched
beneath a dark veil. They looked like a nun who'd sprouted
four heads. The faces stayed still as statues, all looking in the

same direction, though not at me. It unsettled me a bit and I hurried on.

And now these mischievous Loyola girls, whom I consider of modest means, have turned up at a party for rich Sevillians. They must have some kind of relational connection with the wealthy family to be here tonight. Maybe they're just helping out. I'm standing around at a loss when our Genoese hostess, Doña Fillide, appears with her son, Marius. The youth and I size each other up. Age acknowledges its kin. The night will be easier from here on. Marius invites me upstairs to play quoits and I jump at the chance to escape the formalities and frivolities.

I can't mention my near-collision with him in the Giralda. Nor can I ask him about Catarina without giving away my own interest. Ask to see the Rosano aviary? Not without getting him suspicious. One thing I've worked out for myself, thinking about it for weeks since, is that Catarina must have known Marius was going out in the middle of the night. Marius must have told her his intention, and she must have decided to follow him (without letting him know). For some reason she'd held back, decided not to confront him. Or maybe something got in the way of her plans. Maybe I did. Which would explain the theft of my bird. Possibly.

While I play quoits I'm comparing myself with my

long-haired, very feminine opponent. I can see that I don't stand a chance of beating Marius in the appearance stakes. Looking for imperfections I soon find one. Marius has a perverse fascination with the occult. He isn't observing the stars for their own sake; he actually believes the positions of the stars influence the actions of people on the Earth.

I've studied astronomy and mathematics and I know he's talking nonsense. When he mentions a recent visit to the Giralda my ears prick up.

'There was a constellation change happening and I needed to be up high, above the halo of the city, to see it,' he tells me.

Marius is a conversational grasshopper. Now he's asking me which sky sign I'm born under? When I explain I have no idea, Marius says he can work it out from the day of my birth. Born on May thirty-first would make me a Gemini, and so, Marius claims, I will be plagued by inconsistencies because I am fundamentally ruled by a pair of twins.

'Twins? Impossible!' I've lived in the world for sixteen years and I've shown no tendency for division.

'Wait and see. As your life unfolds you will be torn in your allegiances — two women, two vocations, two cities, two countries.'

'Two faiths?' I'm incredulous.

'Perhaps not,' Marius concedes, then launches a new attack.

'I hear you're quite a genius-in-the-making with the Guild of Saint Luke.'

'What do you want me to say?' I reply defensively.

Marius smiles. He wants to know my opinion of the Weddesteeg painting, *The Penitent Woman.*

'Is it as valuable a work as my mother thinks? She paid many escudos for it.'

I shake my head. 'Art cannot be valued in fiscal terms.' This is something I've heard Pacheco say often enough. Marius probably thinks I'm avoiding his question. I cough and continue, trying to make it seem I was just pausing.

'I believe it is the work of a master. It has the stamp of Rome upon it, which makes it valuable here, but in Rome, perhaps less so.'

'Fillide loves the painting.'

He's speaking of his mother, Doña Fillide. And so I can be frank in my admiration.

'It is the white horse that I find remarkable, and the placement of the Morisco standing behind the horse — '

'There's a Morisco in the painting?' Marius raises his eyebrows.

'The monk, yes. He'd have to be Arabic.'

'But the horse is a grey.' It's not a question.

'No, white I think,' I say.

'But you're not sure?' Marius persists.

I hadn't been unsure, but Marius has made me doubtful, damn him.

'Ten maravedís it's a grey,' Marius challenges.

I shake my head and try to laugh it off. I've promised my mother I will never lay a bet if I can help it.

'Let's go downstairs and check,' Marius suggests.

'Where's the painting now?'

'In Fillide's chamber.'

I'd like to look at the painting again so I agree to his suggestion.

Marius and I throw a quoit back and forth as we amble along the upstair's corridor and trundle down the staircase. I nearly fall backwards over the banister when I'm reaching up to catch the high-flying quoit. Honour makes it more important to catch the ring of braided metal, than protect myself from broken bones.

Dancing, music and laughter encroach and part of me wants to go back to the salon where I last saw Catarina and her sisters, but Marius takes me by the arm and leads me to his mother's chamber instead.

The room is pitch black. Marius disappears and returns with a candle-end and a giant candelabra. He places the candelabra on a table and lights six candles. The large painting is standing upright on the floor, resting against a wall. It hasn't been hung as yet.

It's still too dark to decide on the colour of the horse. Marius brings the flaming candelabra right up to the painting. Abracadabra. A horse appears in the room. A tail swishes between muscular flanks. I catch a whiff of manure.

'Mottled-white' we say, almost in unison. I'm relieved I wasn't entirely wrong.

Marius lies down in front of the painting resting on an elbow and cradling the candelabra in his hands. He's posing like a decadent Adonis, his head thrown back. He wants to be in the painting too. He wants to be looked at and admired.

Chimerical flames lick at the bottom portion of the painting, making it look like a scene from Hades.

'Don't flick wax on the painting,' I caution Marius.

'Hmm,' spoken dreamily.

The slightly stealthy atmosphere in the parlour — Doña Fillide could walk in any time — obviously appeals to him.

But I'm suddenly in a bad mood. The painting doesn't look as remarkable as I remember it being. Perhaps I've perjured myself telling Marius it's the work of Rome.

I find another candle and light the wick at Marius's superb triadic holder. I cup the candle in my hand and hold it close to the surface of the painting. Shifting the candle this way and that, up and down, back and forth, searching for clues. I've spent the last four years looking at paintings and I know nearly as much about them as my master, Pacheco.

'Marius,' I say solemnly, 'this is not the Weddesteeg painting. It is a copy.'

'Yes, it is a copy,' agrees Doña Fillide with a rueful smile.

She has left her guests to come looking for Marius, wanting him to take a partner in the dancing.

'So where's the original?' Marius asks, mystified and annoyed.

'In a safer place,' replies Doña Fillide.

'It is a poor imitation,' I say.

Doña Fillide sits down at the table. 'This version was painted by the monk assisting Harmen in the convento,' she explains. 'He's an engraver and a copier of religious art for the Mercedarians.'

She points at the monk in the painting. 'You see him there. Victor María!'

We stare at the figure, matching the name to the face.

Doña Fillide continues: 'Victor María worked on his copy in the evenings. He finished it a short time after Harmen finished the original.'

Just before waking this morning, Doña Fillide tells us, she had a vivid dream. In the dream, the Inquisitor

Zamorana broke into her home. He forced open the French doors and carried *The Penitent Woman* away. Recollection of the dream propelled Doña Fillide into action. She ran downstairs to check her painting was safe. Finding it was, she ran back upstairs, dressed, wrapped her hair in a headscarf, and rushed out onto the street. She only realised she'd lost her beautiful Florentine scarf when she was sitting on a bench in the outer gardens of the palace Alcázar, waiting for Harmen to come down from painting the Duke and his dog. She considered retracing her steps, then gave the scarf up for lost.

Harmen arrived, wiping paint from his hands with a dirty rag. 'He didn't believe in the augury of my dream,' explains Doña Fillide, 'but he said he'd help me out, anyway. He offered to switch the paintings to allay my fears.'

'So there's going to be a burglary tonight, is there?' Marius asks.

'The theft may not happen,' Doña Fillide advises. 'My dream was obviously based on future intent, rather than fulfilled action.'

'Aha,' said Marius probingly, 'and your dream was right, because you *did* lose something. You lost your best scarf worrying about losing something else.'

Fillide Rosano looks deflated when Marius says this. He's being very hard on her. There's an intense familiarity between them. I've not seen the like of this before, between a mother and a grown-up child.

'How'd you know where to find us just now, Fillide?' Marius asks. That casual manner with her again. But there's just the two of them living here in a big house with lots of servants. Marius's wealthy Spanish father passed away some years ago, and he has no living siblings.

'Your painter friend has left a trail of petals,' answers Fillide Rosano and touches me lightly on the arm while pointing to some leaves on the carpet.

Then she claps her hands. Have we forgotten she has a party of guests to attend to? She has no time for further discussion. She insists we both return, so she can assign us dancing partners.

We do as we're told. As we wander back to the dance hall, I'm pondering the strange coincidence between Doña Fillide's fears about Carlos Zamorana (revealed in her dream) and Pacheco's revelations to me about the Dominican prelate. Zamorana has an obsessive interest in the painting. He's been known to destroy 'indecent' artwork in the past, so perhaps it's provident the paintings have been switched.

In the dance hall I find myself slow-skipping in time with an older woman who looks a lot like a giant cake. Her farthingale is enormous and she has a branch of cherries decking her hair. I get her face powder all over my doublet. I'm on the lookout for Catarina again, and before long I catch sight of the Loyola sisters playing in the recesses. My assumption must be correct then. They are here to attend to the guests. To fan the musicians. Massage pinched toes. Scent burning or limp wrists.

I escape into the dining room and partake of the banquet. Then I return to the garden through the gate, retrace my steps and sit on the bench covered in petals. I wait. Glazed by the dampness of night I'm determined to bring on another episode with the girls, this time with the tables turned. Nothing happens. I *will* Catarina to appear. But she doesn't. No-one comes.

Later I return to the house and wander down the corridors searching for Marius, intending to say goodbye. It's not too early to leave and seem rude. Finding myself walking past Doña Fillide's parlour, where earlier Marius showed me the painting, I hear voices and hesitate at the doorway.

Doña Fillide is standing with her back to *The Penitent Woman*, almost touching the canvas. She has placed herself directly in front of the spectre that Weddesteeg calls the human cavity, that dark amorphous shape that supposedly turns up in every painting when it's nearing completion. Fillide Rosano, I notice, is the same size as the shadow;

she fills its dimensions. Indeed she would look good in the painting. It needs a figure to the left of Father Rastro and Paula. The horse, shielding the monk, is heavily prominent on the right.

I hear a sucking sound. There must be a señor in the room with Doña Fillide. Someone's definitely smoking a pipe in there. Perhaps it's Pacheco come to take a look, as I'd predicted. When Doña Fillide starts addressing the table I don't hang around. I don't want Pacheco to take me back to the dance hall with him. I hurry down the corridor and prepare to run up the stairs taking two or three steps at a time. Approaching the staircase I slow down when I notice a bundle lying on the bottom step. Not a drunk I hope. As I carefully step over the body, I recognise Catarina's smallest sister. The body has the even breathing of someone asleep. Further up the stairs another fallen sister is blocking my path. This girl sits up when she hears footsteps.

'Don't,' she says, half asleep.

'Don't what?' I ask.

She still has a mask on. She lifts it and looks at me in confusion then puts it back in place and tries to go to sleep again. This girl has a cushion under her head and is dressed in a big soldier's coat with red lapels.

'I can't get comfortable,' she complains, wriggling about.

At the top of the stairs I expect to find another sister. This sleeping person has a blanket over her head so I can't be sure it's one of the girls, but I recognise the satin slippers. And shapely Loyola ankles. I've seen them, in numbers, frisking round the fishpond. She's either fast asleep, or pretending.

I hesitate at the door of Marius's chamber. There's murmuring inside. The room has a single lantern but is mostly dark. Where are the voices coming from? I can't see anyone in the room. I hear knocking, like wooden clogs, from within the cupboard. People must be inside. Odd sounds like what? Smooching. Long pauses. 'Oh God!' I recognise Marius's voice enthusing. More laughter. Girlish tittering. 'Damn!' Marius again. A slap. Chuckling.

Go looking for love and you can only be humiliated. I go back to the landing. The girl formerly collapsed on the top stair is missing. She's joined her sister on the middle stair. Her hand resting on a weary, slanting head. I'm surprised when she turns around. Catarina? But I don't say her name.

'Did you see Carlotta?' she asks, her tone a little strident.

I stand over them, too flustered to reply. She slides on her backside down to the next stair and shifts over to let me pass.

'One of your younger sisters?' I force the words from my lips.

'Carlotta's older. By a year,' states Catarina. But Catarina is the taller. And the meddler, I'm thinking. The one who wins saddles and blindfolds strangers.

'She was meant to be keeping watch,' Catarina complains.

'Was she? Who was she looking out for?'

'Keeping watch over us, silly.'

'Oh,' I say, staring at the place where Catarina's curly brown wig has come askew from her sleek black hair. She sees me looking at her wet scalp and pulls the wig off, tossing it down the stairs.

'Horrible, hot thing,' she says, and I wonder why she put it on in the first place.

'Did you see Marius Rosano up there?' she asks me bluntly.

'No, I didn't.' I answer with assurance, and quite honestly. So that's why they're sleeping out on the stairs — three young girls swooning over the handsome heir to the Rosano fortune.

I make it to the bottom of the staircase without tripping up and walk back along the corridor, heading for the dining room where the leftovers of the banquet are still on display. I'll have another bite to eat before I head off home.

'Hey, you! Señor,' Catarina shouts. I turn. How could I not? Hanging on her every word.

'What's your name?' she asks, and there's a hint of a taunt in her tone.

If she doesn't know my name then I'm not in the running. That rising lilt means I don't stand a chance. It costs me to ignore her, but I have my pride to protect. I prefer to leave a part of myself behind, a part of my intended future, and walk away, walk on down the corridor of life, past Fillide Rosano who is still standing in front of the painting, this time not alone, but in the arms of Harmen Weddesteeg. I don't stop to take a better look. The embrace of Harmen and Fillide may well have been an end-of-party illusion, I admit, as I was passing by rather quickly, but I continue to recall every detail of my first and only conversation with Catarina de Loyola, memorising forever the rising and dipping scale of her voice, the exact dimensions of her face, the little bit of dark fur above her lip, the eyes shrouded in coal and the beads of sweat on her forehead from the hot and heavy wig. And though I shelve any real expectation of a future with her from this night on, I continue to remember our brief conversation as one of those intense moments when I was on the *inside* of my experience, rather than being an outsider observing others as I feel myself to be most of the time. It didn't end there, where something ended, in the Rosano corridor. It didn't end there because I was to think about her more often, for another year at least, until I made my wedding vows to Juana Pacheco.

CHAPTER FOURTEEN

The Painting 'The Penitent Woman' to Paula Sánchez Comes

I recognise him through a crack in the wooden door. Guido Rizi has pointed the tall Dominican out to me on a number of occasions, though we've never come close to being introduced. When I see Zamorana standing on my doorstep I can only assume he's come to search for the Weddesteeg painting.

Harmen and two of Doña Fillide's servants brought the big painting round here last night. Doña Fillide was tattering ribbons about it, thinking it was going to be stolen by Zamorana. Harmen was in high spirits, and I didn't get the impression he put much faith in Doña Fillide's fears.

'No-one would think to look for it here. You've never met Doña Fillide, have you?'

No, I haven't, but I'm not hiding the censored painting in my house. I don't want to end up in the Castle of the Inquisition, I told him. The screams from that place carry across Triana some days. Harmen argued that I owed him a favour. Had I forgotten the sleepover in the Alcázar palace? Harmen was pretty persuasive last night, and I stupidly gave in.

Of course things didn't work out as Harmen presumed they would. I was taking my breakfast when a messenger arrived at the door. I opened his scroll to find five simple words on the page, with a little picture story to help me understand. Thanks a lot Harmen. The monk's copy of the painting that was put in the real one's place has indeed vanished from the Casa de Rosano overnight. No-one knows who stole it, but Doña Fillide suspects it was Zamorana, as presaged in a dream she had. I put Harmen's scroll in the fire and sat down to think. But I didn't have long to do so because, horror of horrors, here is the thief, hot on the genuine painting's trail. Obviously Zamorana wasn't fooled by the fake. No-one should underestimate this man.

I know I'll have to open my front door to him. And I *do* open it, and there he is, grim beanstalk in an ivory skullcap. He reminds me of a greyhound with his long thin nose.

Tickle him under the arms and he won't laugh or belch as Guido Rizi does. I shouldn't even bother trying. These are not the ones for touching. An *inquisitive* Inquisitor? That's where the name comes from, doesn't it? But he's in some difficulty. Unsteady on his feet, eyes bloodshot. I wonder for a moment if the prelate has been attacked on the street. I'm about to reach out and help him when he collapses onto my doormat and chews on the hem of my gown.

It's a kiss, I realise. He's a skirt kisser. Well I can handle that. A skirt kiss means I'm in the winning seat. But this isn't farce, is it? Am I being mocked? As Zamorana rises from his genuflection, I hold out my hand politely and invite him inside. A trickle of sweat runs down my arm. I wipe it on my dress. I shall refuse to let him search upstairs, I tell myself. I shall say that Bishop Rizi is retiring in my chamber. That he's stark naked. (If nothing else scares Zamorana away the prospect of seeing Rizi nude will.)

But he doesn't want to come inside. His face is so close I can smell his cidery breath. He's drunk, not wounded. He's too inebriated to speak coherently but it sounds like he's asking me for a glass of water. He mumbles something apologetically about taking ill on his way to the Castle.

My maid, at my request, brings him a jug of water and a plate of olives. He drinks the water like a man come out of the desert. He looks at me in fascination, then looks away.

He eats quickly and hungrily. Looks at me, looks away. He's swallowing so quickly he has a coughing fit. 'Violeta, fetch more water.' She returns and waits with me at the door and together we watch him drink. Funny how Violeta knows to do this, to wait, to lend me support. Zamorana's avoided making any formal introductions. If he doesn't ask, then he won't have to acknowledge that he knows who I am. Well, he must know I've a pretty good idea how important *he* is, in his purple silk and all.

I don't invite him in again. His evident weakness has given me strength. He asks for directions back to the bridge. 'His Grace,' I tell Violeta, 'needs assistance returning to the river.' Will she go with him? The pair depart, my maid walking a few yards in front of the eminent priest for propriety's sake.

I close the door and stand with my back pressing against it. I can't work out why Zamorana didn't come inside to look for the painting. As there's been no sign of surveillance, he may not have come for this particular reason. When Violeta returns, I send her off again, this time to inform Harmen about Zamorana's visit. Harmen turns up later in the day, as startled as I am. He puffs on his pipe, thinks about it for a while, then suggests Zamorana may have wished to take a look at the woman who figured in the notorious painting, to size her up in the flesh, so to speak.

'He'd just stolen the painting, so he was feeling excited about it, wasn't he. Going down on his hands and knees, you say. Stinking of cider. He's taken a fancy to you, Paula,' Harmen snorts, but his insensitivity annoys me. I'm sickened by the thought of what Zamorana did to Aurelio, my ladder-man.

'You know the song they sing about Zamorana in the Court of Elms, Harmen? You've only been in Seville a year, so you probably don't. This is how it goes. "Zamorana, man of steel, condemns to die one dozen men; blows his nose, clips his nails, polishes his shoes, for the auto-da-fé is about to begin. Zamorana blows his nose, clips his nails, for one dozen men are about to die."'

I tell Harmen I don't want to keep the painting in my house as it's placing me at risk. Harmen accepts this is true. He even apologises. Doña Fillide will send a coach to collect it tomorrow, he promises, and she will take it directly to her country villa. I shouldn't worry for now. This appeases me a little.

Suddenly I remember. 'What about the monk whose copy has been stolen? Has he been told yet?'

Harmen smiles. 'The sacrifice will have been worth it. Victor María is to become my apprentice.'

'The Mercedarians will let him leave their Order?' I ask, not really understanding why this thought pleases me.

'As my vassal, yes. I'm hoping.'

When Harmen leaves, I go upstairs to check on the painting. I remove the covers and take another look. I sit on my bed and contemplate the images of myself and Enrique Rastro. Yes, this is certainly the original. It's breathtaking. Sensual. Perfect. I admit to taking pleasure in my beauty, but only because Enrique would have taken pleasure in it. I'm interested in him primarily, in my connection to him. Looking at the painting I become wistful about those hot afternoons when I found myself kneeling in front of him. Why does the memory of this intimacy mean so much more than it did at the time? I remember Enrique's sweet respectful smile as he helped me transfer my weight from my knees to my feet before rising. How I would rock back and forth in a squatting position to get my circulation going. He would hold my arm lightly, almost *not* holding it, as we wandered around the studio. 'He touches me, he touches me not.' The monk would be walking the horse in a small half-circle, very close by. Sometimes my free arm would brush against the horse's silky flank. A horsetail would swish against my thigh. The tension in my neck and the numbness of my knees would subside.

With the painting in my possession, I remember again what Enrique looks like. Those round, ruddy cheeks. Those kind, watery-brown eyes. Yes, Harmen has captured him accurately. He isn't handsome but neither is he plain nor really old. I move up close to the painting. My fingers reach out and I trace the coil of rope around Enrique's lower waist. His chalk cassock is flecked with hay-dust. I stroke his ample midriff. He isn't fat, but firmly rounded. Harmen has made him look barn-weary and bed-shy, but it's true that Enrique sometimes *does* look like this. Or he used to.

Pressing the back of my hand against his painted cheek I feel the cool pigment on the canvas, almost skin-like. I imagine his warm cheek and his real mouth, full of blood, pressing against my own. I drop down onto my knees and kiss the thin, colourless lips as best I can. Rastro is kneeling side-on in the painting, so I only have access to half of his body. To half of his mouth.

'And this is what it's like to kiss you,' I say to myself, with the confidence of one whose intended lover is not present to contest the embrace. 'And if I kiss you for long enough, I will bring you to life, here in my sewing room, Enrique Rastro.'

Savouring happy outcomes to my present dilemma I imagine I haven't been rejected after all. I'll see him when he returns from Castile. Perhaps he might even consider breaking his vows with me, no longer a penitent in Purgatory, but merely a woman of Seville, like hundreds of others.

When I'm done making love to the painting, I retrieve my red Magdalen gown from the closet and lay it flat across my bed. Consider it as a seamstress might. Would it be worth mending the cuffs and seams where the fabric has thinned? The rest of the velvet is in prime condition, though I doubt there'll be an opportunity to wear it again in public. But I could wear it around the house; wear it with nothing underneath, luxuriate inside a velvet glove. Perhaps I could even cut it down the middle and turn it into a dressing gown?

It's siesta in Seville and from the top end of town to the bottom, residents have taken to their beds, or are considering doing so. I lie down alongside my dress and tuck a portion of the fabric — where it's still thick — under my cheek. If my heart is no longer measuring time with that of another, it filled up on love during those precious six months in the convento and it'll be keeping me warm for a while yet. I haven't even accepted that my time in the convento is over. I continue to follow instructions, to hear the murmur of men's voices, Harmen and Enrique conversing about the second book of *Don Quixote*, newly in print, which they say is much better than the first. Harmen doing most of the talking, Enrique deferring to the artist, weighing up each reply. I do what Harmen tells me to do, my arms reach out and I grip the base of the wooden Cross 'passionately' as though my life depends on it. I'm putting that Cross to better use than Harmen or Enrique or the red cardinals in Saint Peter's would ever allow. And this is where my dreaming takes me:

'I'm lying across the short beam of the Cross, believing myself to be the short part of the Cross. And Enrique is lying across the long beam of the Cross, believing himself to be the long part of the Cross. First he's lying on his back, then he's lying face down, though we're always pointing in different directions. I've had plenty of time to imagine all the criss-cross possibilities with him and me in different positions along the beams of that Cross. Sometimes on the Cross, sometimes off the Cross. Making diagonal star patterns, with the Cross under our buttocks, lifting our bellies up.

'Either way we join at the middle. Enrique and I. Him on the long arm and me on the short arm, the most conventional way. The short arm is exactly my body length and the long arm is just right for Enrique, with a little extra if he wants to stretch his arms up over his head. Me on my back, him on his front. Belly to belly. This is one for paradise. The long arm and the short arm. Enrique and I. Pinioned to the Cross for pleasure alone.

'Enrique and I are on the Cross and we're going to be lifted up. Yes, we are. A column of angels in wispy white gowns is going to float down and pick us up. Here they come. Soft landings, a gentle whinnying. They flap their cartilage wings and carry us away as we cling to the Cross. (Perhaps our hands are bound to the beams to stop us falling off.)

There are no nails or pins in Limbo. There is no Heaven or Hell, just children and unbaptised souls, and lambs who were born upside down and stayed that way. And now for the first time to Limbo, here come a pair of impossibles like Father Rastro and me. We who have made a game of waiting and kneeling before the big mast of the Cross, as we're doing just now, waiting and not minding waiting.

'I can't see Enrique because he's kneeling behind me, but I can feel the pressure of the damp cloth he's holding against my feet. My bare, dirty feet. I have to soil them in front of him beforehand. He's always about to clean my feet, but he never actually does clean them. I wouldn't let him do that anyway. I wipe them myself before I go home. But he's always *on the point* of cleaning my feet and I'm always *about* to have my feet cleaned by him. And my face has to express an eagerness for absolution with just a tinge of rapture. 'Not only my feet, but my hands and head and my whole body as well.' So saith Simon Peter.

'Enrique and I, joined at the navel. He the long arm and I the short arm. We're holding onto the smooth wooden beams rather than to each other, but his midriff is pressing against mine, and that is a nice place for us to meet. His torso and my torso, transversing around the navel.

I could tell you about a more important place to touch. I could, but it's not what you might think. And so while I'm waiting I'm dreaming that I'm lying across the short beam of the Cross, believing myself to be the short part of the Cross, and Enrique is lying across the long beam of the Cross, believing himself to be the long arm and the righteous hand of God. Which he sometimes is, it's quite true, when he's being the Mercedarian leader. And this is how we pass the Holy hours, on our knees, my only significant passage of time, with him.'

CHAPTER FIFTEEN

Paula and the Ladder-Man are Driven into Exile

It's true, the ladder-man's becoming insubstantial. He's losing his corporeality; transforming into air motes, edgeless and wan. Hair-raising is what I've started calling him. 'Are we going on another *hair-raising* adventure?' I lick him all over to bring him back to life. I conduct fellatio so many times I get swollen lips. He certainly picks up when I do this. But it doesn't last long. Soon I can stab him with my knife and it doesn't hurt. Soon he can't balance on the ladder any more. He can sit weightlessly at the top though, like an angel reclining on a cloud. I have to tie him down before we go to sleep or else he rises to the tin roof and sticks there like a moth.

Other ladder-men seem to be moving into our barrio, taking over his chores. There's an infestation of ladder-men in Triana these days. People can't make a living on the streets any more, so they seek higher pastures. The banging on the roofs at night can be quite alarming. Territorial disputes erupt, and ladder-men give chase to each other like lynxes come down from the forests.

Ladder-men are falling from the roofs in their battles. Joining the bumps of pumpkins in kitchen gardens. The residents of Seville want the men off their properties, purged from the skyline, rid from their flowerbeds. The ladder-man excess means they've become less popular. Fading are the days when the gentle twilight shepherds were held in high esteem. Then, before we know it, fading into oblivion are the ladder-men themselves. All of them, walking south in a long procession, like the Moriscos leaving Seville after hundreds of years in our midst.

'If you're going, can I come too?'

'You're not a ladder-man, and ladder-women don't count,' he writes on his slate. Constantly reading Aurelio's notes has taught me letters.

'But Hortense. She had a ladder necklace.'

'She probably made it herself,' he writes on the palm of my hand with a reed pen.

'You'll have to touch earth to go down there,' I say, hoping to change his mind.

'A gang from the guild will lend me a hand,' he explains in mime.

'I want to come too.'

Aurelio puts his arms around me. He's all jutting hips and bony pelvis.

I stick my hand inside his ribcage and hold onto his heart. It feels like a poached quince. His heart pulses in my hand like his penis used to do when he was aroused.

'You can come along for the ride,' he allows.

Which means, I suppose, that I miss out on the fun at the end of the journey.

But I join the caravan posthaste, travelling light with a few belongings and a tent. No mules or horses allowed. Our penance will be to walk like pilgrims. Just some ladder-girl strays like me and a fair few wives and children in attendance. A ladder-man whose name I don't know carries a cat on his shoulders, birdlike. In Santa María this fellow was the rooftop king of cats. He fed and pampered hundreds, or so I'm told.

Four ladder-men pick up Aurelio's ladder keeping it flat and horizontal. Aurelio climbs directly from a friend's pony onto the ladder. He's a sultan lounging on a litter. I hold a sunshade over his head to protect him from inclement weather. The journey begins and we follow the bends of the river south.

The caravan travels for three days, along the fertile Guadalquivir valley. We pass almond groves and olive farms. Peasants planting and pruning greet us in concern. Perhaps they think we are mourners returning from a funeral in Seville. What do they know that we don't?

At end of day we lay down in the fields alongside sheep and goats. Aurelio and the ladder-men prefer to sleep up high, on hayricks or in the lofts of stables. In the morning we join Bartolomé, a former parish priest, for prayers then step fully clothed into the river to wash. Even Aurelio. As long as he doesn't touch the sandy bottom he says he feels okay. He avoids his 'terror'. If I knew what everyone calls his 'terror' was, I would try to cure him.

When the river is flowing quickly we get on our ladders and float downstream instead of walking. Ladders make good rafts and you can stick your hand down and pull out a fish if you're fast enough. Aurelio stands on his ladder while we're drifting along the water. He's no fool; he has attained the art of perfect balance. Others copy him, which makes the rest of us 'clingers on' feel very incompetent.

We go back to walking when the river veers the wrong way. Aurelio dries his clothes standing on his ladder in the stream of a windmill. The fan of the windmill ruffles his shepherd's shift. He can catch the wind like it's falling rain or strands of whipped sugar. He catches a stream of wind in his hands and cupping it tightly, gives it to me. I smile and take it from him. I feel the wind spinning inside the bowl of my hands, the wind using up its energy. It makes a sigh when it's spent.

We stand on a stile beneath the windmill and I copy him. My skirt rises up and flaps in my face. Then I jump off the stile and pretend to fly like we used to do as children. I collect sticks and vines and Aurelio crafts for me a little windmill. He skewers leaves with the sticks. I hold my windmill up to the air as I'm walking along, combing the air with the twirling leaves. The toy mill whistles and whirrs. I blow on it with my mouth and it rasps like corn husks.

Closer to our destination Aurelio doesn't bother with the ruse of the litter any more. He lets it be known he can levitate himself off the ground. I continue to carry his ladder and sack for him, walking with a ladder over each shoulder (his and mine) while Aurelio drifts along beside me. Sometimes he floats horizontal like an eel. In daylight it's hard to see him, but at night he shines luminously, giving off a warm copper glow. Up in a loft we join hands and my body becomes burning rock, straight out of a volcano. I turn to liquid as we make love, then harden back into myself, copper running through my veins.

We've been walking along the riverine valley for some days, me kicking autumn leaves out of the way, Aurelio looping trees, pulling late season fruit from the top branches, when our procession of exiles takes a detour uphill. Our caravan passes one whitewashed village after another. The road is busy with travellers. Lots and lots of ladder-men. We pass some returning from our destination. Ladder-men wrapped in blankets with singing children hanging onto them. And weeping wives in black. Silent stragglers.

'There's the possibility for renewal,' Aurelio writes on his slate after I've tied him down for the night. There is the possibility, he repeats, and then there isn't. You go all the way up and you mightn't come back. I'm going to have to take the chance. (He's writing to himself rather than to me for a change and that's a worry.)

We come to an open plain with birds flying straight upwards. A shiver runs down my spine. Before long we meet a sign that reads, 'Climb at your own cost', and then further on down the track, another: 'Let dead souls go'.

I see where everyone's heading. Far away in the distance a thin pillar or pole rises up to the clouds. As we get closer I can see it's not a pillar, but a giant palm tree, made of very strong wood, so tall it couldn't be one tree, it would have to be hundreds joined together. And there are creatures moving up the long tree in columns, like ants.

We march closer. It's not a tree but a ladder with rungs and there are angelic forms climbing up to Heaven. Hundreds of them, disappearing through the roof of the sky. And a few, I notice, are coming back down the other side of the stairway, very slowly, stopping to bump noses with those going up. How very peculiar.

This is the stem of the Earth, I think. This is the place where we are joined to the sun and the moon, like an apple is joined to the rest of the tree.

Aurelio and I pass by a field of tents. Families prodding fires, cooking soup. Children running about with straggly hair. Some are sitting and playing a game in the soil. Knucklebones we called it in my village.

'Waiting for their ladder-men to return,' explains Aurelio, in a sign language I've become familiar with. He's looking grim and I'm feeling grim in expectation. Files of anxious women line the path like pine trees. When a frostbitten man with white whiskers lumbers past, two women run forward and embrace him, shrieking in delight.

Getting closer to the giant ladder I can see that the climbers are not really angels as they don't have wings. I know who they must be. They are ladder-men on their final mission.

We cross a ring of water a couple of metres wide, but shallow. I only get my feet wet. Then we clamber over a barrier of giant egg-shaped stones. Purple and mauve like the inside of mussel shells.

We have to walk through what in hindsight I think must have been an optical illusion. It's a ring of fire, six feet high. There's a magician of sorts who stands on the other side of the fire. He uses a scythe to sweep the flames back and let us pass. He has no fear and neither do we, walking through the gap in the flames. (Not a hair on my body is singed.)

And now comes a rope that is intended to keep wellwishers back. It is here we must part. I can go no further, but I may linger for a short while. A man has come to weigh Aurelio. He has to be light to make his ascent. 'So the ladder doesn't lean.'

'Someone is going to fall,' I say in agitation, looking up, expecting to see a man tumbling down at this very moment.

The measurer shakes his head. 'It rarely happens.'

'What is your weight these days?' I ask, and Aurelio shakes his head. He'll be too light to measure.

'No gravity, no weight,' the measurer tells Aurelio with approval. 'So you're going up directly. You won't need to fast.'

'Better to follow the chain of men,' a voice behind us says. The papal edict: mount the ladder with Jacob or else.

Somewhere else there must be a sign, I'm sure, that says, 'Don't miss your chance of returning'.

My ladder-man is embracing me goodbye, but his body is so wasted he has already half-departed. There's to be a victory of sorts, and suddenly I know what it is: it is the strength of my love returning from childhood. It's as if it has been held in some carved tree-trunk all this time and it's suddenly been released; the raw lovely feeling of being seven and eight comes rushing back to me. I emerge long-limbed from a white crib, clutching the three stones that (used to) make Aurelio and me the same weight, even though I'm twenty times heavier than the wafer he has become. We are the same weight in feeling, and that is rare.

And Aurelio departs into the void that is also the resting-place of my mother, somewhere up above, beyond.

The rope is open and Aurelio is approaching the forbidding ladder that rises up to the sky. There's a queue of people behind me, so I can't stand here any longer. I make my way back across the circles of fire and stone and water and it is here, on the dusty path, that I pause and watch my ladder-man begin his ascent. I feel quite composed, almost proud. But there are so many climbing today and I soon lose sight of Aurelio.

I'm surprised that I don't feel weepy. What wondrous man is this who's healed a wound, not furrowed one open? Even in parting he's withdrawn himself, yet not his affection. I return to the holding fields and find an empty spot to camp. In three days, there will be a chance for his renewal. And after that you can wait and wait, so they tell me. After a week the ladder-men never return. Or if they do it's a miracle. Whatever happens up in the clouds they will either return to flesh or decompose in air. It's a question of mental resistance, so say those returning with rounded flesh. It's an exquisite feeling to turn into air. Your body becomes a lyre and you feel music running through the threads of your being. It's better than the best lovemaking, they say. Who would return to us after knowing such ecstasy? Only those who can bind flesh to their bodies. Attach themselves to sheets of ice until their bodies harden and thicken again. It is very painful apparently, to bind oneself to ice, and most escape the torture for the freedom of the lyre, so say those who have endured and returned to us whole.

So I sit on our two ladders with my chin in my hands and wait. Some of the women I know from our caravan are waiting too. We look to the ladder in the sky, even when it's too dark to see. On the second evening, when I know the time is ripe for either his return or his mourning, I light a candle and keep a vigil by the path with the other women. There is sporadic shrieking. Rapturous reunions follow. One of the men from our caravan has returned. We womenfolk run to embrace him. He's frozen solid and walking very stiffly. We warm him by a fire, hold him till he cries and thaws. He can't tell us anything yet. His teeth are chattering. His body shaking. His hair and skin are drained of colour.

Eventually he tells us that there were pale-blue angels up there who ran swords through the ladder-men's bodies. The men leaked orange blood but they didn't die. The angels lured the men to their glittering landscapes to sleep with them. He said he'd never met such licentious women. 'They do it with anyone. No matter how cold you are; they want you.' It was a huge place, the returning man said, with snow cathedrals and a high-pitched ringing glare that hurt both your ears and eyes. The colours were so sharp that after a while he lost sight of everyone he knew. (He was sorry, but he couldn't tell us what happened to the other ladder-men in our caravan.) There were some nice angels, he admitted, who handed out sugar crystals.

When the returning ladder-man has regained his normal complexion, he has to go through the ritual burning of his ladder. Or so the authorities decree. Back in Seville he will never again be seduced by the lure of rooftop balconies. The man says he feels cured already. But the ladder-burning ritual must go ahead.

Later that night I hear the returned ladder-man's wife sobbing in the tent beside mine. 'You're not the man you used to be.' I am quietly perturbed. But the next day I wake in anticipation. This is the day my Aurelio has to return, or he will never do so. I stand alert on the track and keep a look out for his rake-like physique. As day dies I know any chance of seeing him again is unlikely, but I force myself to be happy for him. He will become a lyre of the air and hear the music running through his veins. Forever.

But I wish he'd survived the sword-thrusts of angels and was returning frozen yet replenished. Or even unreplenished. I'd take him back in any condition or shape. As I watch the slow trickle of unfamiliar ladder-men, I've almost given up hope when I see someone who makes my heart skip. It is someone I am close to, but oddly, I can't remember who he is. Then I realise it's Enrique Rastro, but he isn't forty years old anymore. He is very young, about twenty-five. I begin to wander along the wet track, just behind him, trying to get a better look but not wanting to seem rude. He notices me after a while and stops.

'Enrique?'

'Do I know you from somewhere?' His voice is Enrique's, though not as world-weary as I remember.

'You look so young.'

Enrique shrugs and keeps walking slowly. He is surely in some pain.

I run after him and clutch hold of his arm, 'Enrique! It's me Paula.'

He turns halfway round and says sorry, politely, but shakes his arm a little to release my hold. My hand has stuck to his sleeve through the contact of ice. Not until the ice breaks does my hand drop away. It is a little awkward hanging on to him when he doesn't want me to.

It is plainly obvious that this Enrique look-alike doesn't know who I am. What a rebuff. Nor is he affected by the spell of my beauty, like the older Enrique was. It can't be Enrique. Unless it is 1600 again and everything has been cast back, as happens in dreams or at the theatre.

We're standing looking at each other and I say, 'What was it like up there?'

'Apart from the blue angels, pretty boring.'

'Did you meet someone called Aurelio by any chance?'

He forces a tolerant smile. 'Look. I don't think I know you, but thank you for your interest.'

He has no memory of me and he isn't pretending. It must be Enrique though, turned back in time. This might explain why he doesn't know me. Because we haven't met yet. It still has to happen in the future.

A couple more ladder-men are trudging down the path, returning from their exploits in the sky, and I turn back to see if Aurelio is among them. I get caught up in the crush of a family reunion. By the time I remember Enrique again he is tiny in the distance. I have some of his icy wetness still on my hand and I put my fingers in my mouth and suck on them. Sugar crystals, for sure.

There's a chance, one in a million, that Aurelio may still return. I'm prepared to face reality though, so I ready myself for departure. Before I leave the campsite I decide to throw our two ladders on the bonfire. I don't want to have to lug them home and I'd have to sneak them into Seville if I did. Ladders are out of favour, along with their owners, and you need a costly licence to carry one around. I throw both on the fire and hear the nails pop like firecrackers, but I keep the bells, tying them together with the handkerchiefs and hanging them round my neck. I join the depleted caravan returning to Seville and, as I walk, I jangle like a cow, which keeps the predators from my side during the day and away from my tent at night.

When I'm back in Triana I find a note to me in Aurelio's bundle of belongings. It says, 'Don't forget that ladder-men don't always come back looking the same.' And on the other side of the parchment, 'Why don't I like to touch earth? They buried me in soil to make me confess.'

But he never told me about his tongue. And I never confessed to knowing. He wouldn't want me to think he'd been degraded and mutilated like that.

The young Enrique continued to plague my thoughts. Had Father Rastro gone up the great ladder instead of going to Castile? Had the encounter with angels and ice made him look so young? No, it couldn't have been he who I met. Enrique's not a ladder-man; he couldn't join the guild and he wouldn't be driven to climb up there.

There are great ladders in other places apparently. (Bartolomé, a member of our caravan who made it back down safely, told me.) Sometimes people go down the wrong ladders on their return journey. There was a frozen Chinaman who came down the track in Andalucía. He didn't know where he was and we tried to help him out. Some of our men may have got lost in the sky above and gone down a ladder to Russia or China. There's a chance Aurelio went down the wrong ladder. Some men turn up a year or more later having found their way home, like lost cats.

Back in Seville a letter arrives from Rome. I open it in expectation, but am quickly disappointed. It's only from Bishop Rizi. I attempt to read it to myself. My benefactor says he's given up on me. He has returned to Rome, his birthplace. I've resisted his advances one time too many.

So be it. The house stays mine, but with no income flowing in, I shall have to give up Violeta and do more artist modelling.

The next day I visit Harmen who hadn't even realised I'd gone away. Is Father Rastro *really* in Castile as I've been told? Harmen says he knows from Doña Fillide, whom he is to wed next week, that Father Rastro is currently residing in his birthplace of Toledo. Rastro's mother died last month, Harmen explains, and he had to leave in a great hurry to attend her funeral. (So I only got told a piece of the story in the convento!)

I'm left to my own devices. Abandoned (once again) by the important men in my life. Harmen, whom I've been able to call my friend, soon to be married. Enrique, my spiritual advisor — whom I admit to loving — mourning his mother up north. Rizi, my benefactor, gone for good. Aurelio, my teacher in the art of loving, still missing, believed to have expired in a cloud.

I don't feel like getting any replacements. I sit on my balcony and watch for Aurelio as I used to do in the evenings before the ladder-man plague began.

'Have you seen the ladder-man?' I ask the only neighbours I've got to know, the ones whom I used to chat with while they were bird-watching.

'Long gone now. But climb over for a coffee, dear.'

Sometimes I do. And keep up my search. Scan the roofs for his hairpin shape. Nothing much stirs on the balconies these days. The cats and birds are noisier. Wilder for feed than before. Like me, they miss our ephemeral friend.

'He was just a phantom, wasn't he?' I lament.

'And what if he was?' console my neighbours. 'He was a quiet one, but diligent; we liked him as much as you did.'

'You did? That's nice,' I say, leaning forwards and hugging my knees hard against my chest, taking physical comfort in their pressure. Why aren't I sad? Why haven't I cried? I still don't know. But something's going to happen, I feel sure. Orange copper flowing through my veins; hayloft chatter of leaves in my head. Love is a flame that continues to burn, within if not without.

CHAPTER SIXTEEN

The Flight of the Moriscos

*As recounted by Diego Velázquez nearing the end of
the year of our Lord, 1616*

Brazenly and even carrying some of their belongings with
them, the Morisco boys walked out of the front gate in
broad daylight, telling the guard of the Holy Brotherhood
they were on a mission for Father Lopez. The friars were
busy organising a Saint's Day procession, so the Moriscos'
absence wasn't noticed until evening. But the boys were
only two miles from Seville when Camilo changed his
mind about the adventure. He slouched back home with
his friends' accusations of 'coward' and 'turncoat' sticking

in his back. Mercedarian scouts were sent out, and the others were caught napping before dawn of the next day.

The second time, the boys escaped by hiding in a milk dray while the driver of the cart was chatting to one of the seminary cooks. It was still dark when the dray left the convento grounds. As it slowed to turn a corner, the boys jumped out and ran down a side alley. They were caught two days later, trying to sell a Mercedarian icon to a priest standing in the patio of a church in San Gil.

The third time, the boys concocted a more cunning plan. It was All Saints' Day and they begged to be allowed to join the procession. They marched alongside cardboard giants, tar-faced demons and flagellating mystics. They sang their hearts out, not knowing whether they would get a chance to bolt or not. Luck came to their aid. A fight broke out between two cutlass-wielding spectators, the boys signalled to each other and broke from formation, running away in five different directions. Father Lopez was spinning around like a weather vane trying to keep track of the five. Camilo was able to tell the Moriscos this amusing fact much later, because he didn't run away with the others. Luis, Telmo, Arauz, Benito and Remi met up again on the docks as planned, having evaded detection so far. Little fools, they applied for work on the galleys, intending to earn their passage to Tunis. While they were being weighed and measured, they were intercepted by a burly customs official.

'Kid, I recognised you straight away,' the official scolded Luis, and the boys were roped together and led back to captivity.

'I'm going to die of shame,' Luis told his friends.

'Don't worry. Selling images of yourself is only an offence in Muhammadan lands,' comforted Telmo.

The sketches I made of Luis two years ago had been put to good use by the ecclesiastical sheriffs. Luis's face had been copied again and again and distributed to checkpoints around the town. The authorities were all familiar with the sweet round face of the biggest Morisco. News of the boys' capture spread from the convento to the Court of Elms. While Sevillians generally have no liking for Moriscos, the fact that the escapees were so young elicited sympathy for their cause.

Back on Mercedarian land, acting leader Lopez was getting flustered. Victor María, still residing in the convento, was instructed to paint a group portrait of the Moriscos. This portrait would be copied and circulated around town. Victor María told Harmen Weddesteeg that he was going to do the portrait a professional injustice.

'They look nothing like the real boys!' Father Lopez exclaimed on seeing the near-finished portrait, and

Victor María, stalling for time, apologised for his lousy rendering.

'I'm a novice painter, but I'll keep on trying.'

Father Lopez wanted an accomplished painter to be brought in to do the job, and there was even some talk of it being me (can you believe it?) though no-one actually approached me on the matter. The boys were warned they'd have to make their next move fast.

They scaled a convento wall on a moonless night, separated into two groups and left Seville on foot. Luis and Benito were beaten up by bandits a few miles from town. They were left bleeding on the road. Two Christians on horseback rode by and carried them to a nearby Loreto convent, where the boys met up with two Morisco girls, one of them who turned out to be Benito's twin sister. A happy reunion ensued, but the Loreto nuns had no qualms about returning the missing boys to the priests. They sent a messenger to Father Lopez with news of the boys' interception.

Remi and the Cordoban brothers were at large for a longer time, but Arauz had injured his ankle springing down from the high convento wall. As a consequence the three of them were forced to find a place of rest not far from town. The boys accepted work in the apple orchards, hoping to make a little money and live on apples, but they were not far enough from Seville to evade detection. After ten days, they too ended up back in the convento, disappointed, but not dejected. Camilo, who had stayed behind each time after the first, let out war-whoops of delight when he saw his friends enter the cloister courtyard. Later on, reunited in the dormitory, Camilo hugged each of them for a long time.

'You didn't make it!'

Luis ruffled his hair and told him they intended to try once more.

'Do you like my new glasses?' Camilo asked.

Luis and Benito both tried the pair of glasses on. They claimed they couldn't see a thing and the lenses hurt their eyes.

After the fourth failed attempt, the younger boys decided that they had sound reasons to stay in the convento, in particular four meals a day and soft beds to sleep in at night, but the olders boys, Luis and Telmo, were still intent on leaving.

I wasn't privy to any of their escape attempts. I learned about the boys' misadventures from reading the broadsheets, listening to gossip and then, much later, the full story with all the details from Luis de Pareja himself.

It was on one of my afternoon strolls about the town that I recognised his picture nailed to the walls of the

Arenal. The picture on display was a copy of my drawing of Luis laughing, the one I did nearly two years ago. Why the authorities chose this drawing to rein the boys in I don't know, but I assumed it was because they thought it was the closest likeness.

I remember making Luis laugh that afternoon in Pacheco's studio when he was disinclined to do so, and now Luis is being referred to in the broadsheets as 'the laughing Morisco', as though this is true to his nature, to laugh at life, to laugh in the face of adversity, to laugh as he boards the galleys to row his way to freedom, as though he's enjoying every moment of his wing-clipped existence.

A day or two after hearing about the Morisco boys' injuries, I ran into Paula Sánchez in San Vicente Square.

'Paula!'

'Diego Velázquez, how fortunate!'

We hadn't seen each other for a couple of months.

Paula started to explain why she hadn't been able to help Luis, as I'd asked her to do, on that sweltering afternoon when I was possessed by a desire to pass by her home.

'Enrique Rastro has been in Toledo for some time,' Paula said. 'When Father Lopez took charge, he immediately put an end to my visits.'

She didn't need to explain; I knew Father Rastro had been up north and I didn't blame her for anything. The

Inquisition guards, she continued in her defence, came to her house last time the boys escaped. They searched inside. They were rough brutes, she said, in disgust. They ripped up her carpets. They pierced her mattress with their swords. When her black slave protested, they knocked her against a wall and laughed when she cried.

Paula's heard that the Morisco boys have been apprehended a fourth time. Did I know anything about their current situation?

I didn't mention the boys' alleged injuries. I didn't want to alarm her. I volunteered to visit the boys and find out how they were faring. Paula brightened on hearing this. And could I give them some money from her, clandestinely? Yes, I was surprised to hear myself say, I will do that, if I can.

She made me promise, she handed the money over, a generous amount, so I guess I'll have to.

'And if Enrique Rastro has come back,' Paula stammered. 'Shall I tell him something, if he's back?'

'No, no. Please don't mention me. Just let me know later, if he has returned.'

I put two and two together.

'Is it good for you, if he's back?' I inquired.

Paula shook her head. 'Not for me it isn't. At least, not if he's been back for a while.'

I nodded understandingly. I've guessed correctly, but more importantly, Paula has let me share in her secret. I've got this thing about people not trusting me, so it means a lot that this exceptional woman does.

I arrive at the convento with the money from Paula and a gift that Juana Pacheco has made at my request — a parcel of sugared egg whites, a confection popular among children. It seems from what I can infer at the gate that Father Rastro is still away in the north.

Father Lopez is accommodating, but he will only grant me access to Luis.

'Why do you want to see the others?'

At the last moment he changes his mind and allows Benito to come along too.

'They're not to be treated as celebrities,' Father Lopez quibbles as the boys enter the room. 'Don't put more ideas into their heads than they already have.'

Straight away Luis unbuttons his cassock to show me his injuries. Obviously he thinks this is what I've come to see. Others have done so apparently.

'These are knife wounds!' I'm squatting down and fingering the abrasions on his legs and back. Only when he has had his full of my sympathy does he let me turn my attention to Benito who is more of a fright. He has scabs on his face, and his hair has been shaved to tend a nasty wound. His shaved head makes him look a bit like an old man.

'So you copped it too?' I say, stating the obvious, trying hard not to smile.

Benito nods and proudly rubs his hand over his shorn head. Then the two boys, as though on cue, perform little actions and acrobatics in front of me, to explain what happened. Benito echoes everything Luis says, so the story goes like this:

'One of them has Benito on the ground and is knocking his head against the flagstones,' Luis begins.

'Yes, he's knocking my head against the flagstones.'

'And I get the bastard in the kidneys,' says Luis.

'Harun Luis kicks him in the kidneys.'

'The bastard squeals and rolls over like he's going to die.'

'Yes, like he's going to die,' says Benito, acting out the torment of the villain with much enthusiasm.

'And I whack him in the eyes with my bag.'

'You sock me, *him* I mean, with your bag, just like that.'

'The other lashes me with his knife,' Luis says, as Benito rises from his prostration and pulls a chimerical dagger out of his clothing.

'And blood spurts everywhere,' Benito finishes off by

lunging at Luis's back and legs and thrusting, thrusting, thrusting countless times and surely killing his victim if this were real life.

'Red, red gouge,' Benito inveighs slowly and solemnly, turning to me and bringing the performance to a close.

Red, red gouge indeed. The boys have portrayed themselves as courageous, but I wonder what really happened during the assault.

At this point I remember Paula's gift, and ask if we may go out into the courtyard to eat Juana's treat. I hold her parcel of sweets up for inspection and Father Lopez takes a peek at the messy meringues and permits us to leave. In the garden Luis makes for an enormous fig tree and when we're hidden under its low-lying boughs I hand over the confections. Not realising they're to share with the other Moriscos, Benito and Luis pop them in their mouths in quick succession.

'Paula Sánchez has asked me to convey her warmest sympathies to Telmo and Arauz,' I quietly inform the boys.

I pick up a papery brown fig leaf and slip the knuckle bag that's hiding Paula's coins beneath it. I shift the big leaf slowly across the grass. 'And she also gives you, *all of you Moriscos that is*, a gift.'

Luis accepts the fig leaf knowingly and nonchalantly, enfolding crumbly leaf and bag securely in his clothing without saying a word of thanks. This is probably because he's still chewing egg whites and also because he couldn't know how much money is in the bag with the knucklebones.

'Paula says not to come to her home if you escape again. They searched for you there last time.'

As he's almost finished munching, Luis manages a reply. 'The Castle guards are watching from the gallery and roof. The fence is guarded with dogs and they bark if we come close; then the guards yell at us.'

'Don't let the guards apprehend you for they will show you no mercy,' I tell him.

I can't think of anything encouraging to add, so I fall back on what I'm not supposed to say. 'Did you know you boys are the talk of the town?'

'Will anyone be painting us again?' Luis replies sarcastically, with intended meaning.

He's referring to Victor María's doltish efforts with the paintbrush. My response is to laugh and Luis starts laughing too. Laughter as freedom — the freedom to laugh. The Moriscos getting their own back.

Victor María left the convento soon after his botched effort with the group portrait. Now he's vassalled to Harmen Weddesteeg who's apparently negotiating a new legal status for the self-exiled monk. There have been all sorts of difficulties because Victor María has no civil status; he's someone officially owned by the Church. Marius Rosano, who seems to keep regular counsel with Weddesteeg these days, told me all about it. Marius has been staying with the newlyweds in their country villa. While in Carmona, Marius saw Harmen set up his easel and alter the painting known as *The Penitent Woman*. The place once occupied by the human cavity has been filled by a woman in a grey and pink dress holding open an olive-green fan. Doña Fillide herself! Well, she has the perfect dimensions for it.

After leaving Luis and Benito in the convento, I wander the chilly streets of San Vicente and San Pedro without the usual decisiveness in my gait. I'm a broken compass of sorts. Not sure where to go or what to search for. I'll seek out Paula Sánchez tomorrow or the next day. Find her in the marketplace, accompanied by her black slave. Tell her the boys are doing well. That they're joking about their misfortunes.

I pull my hat down over my ears protectively and order some roasted chestnuts from a street vendor. This gives me a chance to stand quietly beside the brazier and attend to a runny nose. These well-intentioned visits to the convento could be my undoing. It's quite possible the Mercedarians will find out I gave Luis all that money. Pacheco might come to hear of it, and he wouldn't be impressed.

The Moriscos have surely made their final escape from the convento. The injuries they sustained and the Inquisition guards will deter them in future.

My own affairs seem blighted. Since the intriguing episode with the scurrilous nymphs in the Casa de Rosano, I haven't sighted Catarina de Loyola. The party was months ago now. The rumour is that Catarina has been taken by the smallpox. She's been convalescing in another town, I've heard, but she may be returning soon. If she's ill, I hope she recovers, and unscathed. Her skin could be ruined, her impulsiveness curtailed.

After the Rosano party, I took my chance and asked Marius about Catarina. Believing his interest was with the older sister, Carlotta, made it easier to broach the topic. Marius didn't give me a direct answer; 'Ah, lovely Catarina de Loyola,' was all he would say. Perhaps he's working his way through all the sisters. It was beneath my dignity to plead with him to tell me more, so I've been left surmising. I have no idea if Marius knows *everything* about Catarina or *nothing* about her and just likes being enigmatic. The latter wouldn't surprise me. I dislike him for his smug obliqueness either way. Since then — well *as* has been the case all along if I were to be strictly honest — our friendship has been one-sided, with Marius making all the overtures.

He's invited me to watch the lunar eclipse from the top of the Giralda tonight. It's going to be a clear night, the changes on the moon's surface will look wondrous through his refractive telescope, but in spite of my genuine desire to witness the spectacle, I've declined the offer. I'll spend the evening with my family in San Pedro and hope they cheer me up.

CHAPTER SEVENTEEN

In Triana, Paula Observes an Astronomical Wonder

Someone has pricked my arm gently with a pin. No, it's not a pinprick. It's a needle of light entering the room. Is it really the middle of the night? I slip out of bed cautiously, so as not to disturb my lap-dog Alanis. Walk to the window, open the curtain and drown for a moment in silver spray. 'Moonbathing' Aurelio used to call it: 'Stand under a creamy fountain and you realise you're alive.' Or did the moon tell me that?

The lunar light is so exceptional I wonder if the sun isn't shining *through* the moon. Suddenly I feel completely awake, days away from sleep. Draping a shawl about my shoulders, I climb up to my roof-garden to take a closer look at the night. Seville is experiencing a cold snap, but I'm still warm from bed.

I sit in an iron chair and pull my shawl around me. I can't help but look straight up at the moon. A crescent-shaped shadow has covered the edge of the sphere. I've seen nothing like this before; I know of no explanation for the abnormality.

A breeze is blowing and the wavy sea of nearby palm fronds is tickling my legs. Beneath my flannel nightdress my nipples are tingling. A cat is moving across the roof of an adjoining house. It's my own cat Maio, who found his way back to me last month by good fortune, after they closed the citadel of balance. The cat jumps down from a ledge, slinks up beside me and rubs its fur against my bare legs. It's a silver cat, I'm thinking, but when I lean down to pat it, I notice the fur is ginger-brown. The cat's soft fur rubbing back and forth across my calves arouses me too.

Murmuring voices drift across the terraces. Through the screen of palm fronds, I observe my neighbours sitting at a table and drinking what smells like freshly ground coffee. I wonder if they're celebrating an anniversary to be sitting outside in the cold. I'm grateful to be hidden from them by an awning as well as the plants. I'm glad to have their company, but I don't really want them to know I'm up here at such an ungodly hour.

Bats fly past on the way to the Alcázar gardens, their wings tinted pink in the curdled moonlight. Are they bats, or some other flying creatures? I watch their spectral path north. The gingerbread tower looms in the distance. The Giralda's more than just a silhouette tonight. Flickering candlelight emanates from the minaret. What could be going on up there?

Time passes. I shift further back in my chair and focus on the moon again. It's definitely waning at a very rapid pace. Slowly and with mathematical precision the left side of the moon is being drained of its translucent whiteness.

I imagine the moon signalling to me, trying to warn me, 'I'm predicting a coming plague, a biblical flood, the long-expected Turkish invasion . . . '

As dire possibilities drift through my mind the moon keeps receding, leaving only a dull russet husk behind.

If the moon dies, what will happen to the earth? Only a pencil-thin curve of brightness remains. 'Oh, you poor sick thing!' I whisper in fascination.

I pull my knees up to my chest to keep warm and suck on the tassel-ends of my shawl. I often suck on a sleeve or on the edge of a face towel in private, for comfort. I keep an eye on my neighbours. They're watching the night sky too, and judging from their intermittent laughter, they're not alarmed by what they're seeing. If they're not worrying, neither should I.

As I concentrate on the ailing moon my ears become finely tuned. Perfectly tuned, I'll think later on, trying to explain it. I can hear speaking nearby, but it isn't coming from the adjacent balcony. A word-capsule transported on the wind. In the breeze I can make out a man's voice speaking a tongue I don't know. He's saying, over and over, a word that sounds like *kleipsis* or even *ekleipsis*, but I don't know what this means. Then I hear Enrique Rastro, but he sounds far away, whereas the first voice is close beside me. Enrique is saying 'abandonment' as though translating. Then I hear both voices. Enrique's faintly echoing, and the foreign one that is close: 'The attachment is no longer yours.'

Coming quickly after this lunar parable a scroll-size image of Enrique Rastro appears. He's walking along a country road, pulling a horse by a leather lead. The road is unmade and Enrique and the horse are hobbling along. The horse is most resistant. Then without warning, the horse and man tumble into a ditch, one after the other. The horse clambers out and gallops away, disappearing into a field of tall wheat. When the horse emerges from the wheat, it's bearing two riders, but the riders have their backs to me and I can't be sure who they are. I feel the female rider to be myself, but the male rider isn't identifiable. Then the horse and its riders, and the scroll floating before me on which the picture is painted, all disappear.

I hope Enrique is all right. It's not propitious to fall in a ditch. I look to the moon for help, but it doesn't send another scroll-picture. Perhaps it feels as bereft as I do.

'Thank you, moon,' I say solemnly. Something has been abandoned. Not just the dependable lunar presence. Something in myself. I feel elated for a moment, then tearful; I hear my heart throbbing in my breasts and further down in my womb and sexual organs.

Later there's cheering from the adjacent balcony. I open my eyes, look at the sky, and understand. A crescent moon of brilliant intensity has awoken on the gutted sphere; our celestial neighbour is coming back into existence.

The word-capsule and floating image may have been full of instructional meaning, but I'm too attached to the past to care about the imminent future. The man galloping away with me on the horse? Well, it didn't *look* like him, but it would have to be Enrique, wouldn't it? No-one else matters.

I wait on the balcony for a full revival. I see a shooting star, then another. It's all happening in the sky over Seville tonight. The nape of my neck is damp, my extremities are freezing. I ease up from the chair and climb back down the ladder, my feet so numb I can't feel the steps. In my bedchamber I search out some stockings and pull them on my feet, and also on my hands. 'I'm webbed,' my teeth chatter, as I clamber under the covers.

Alanis sighs mournfully and shifts position at the end of the bed. Lays his head upon my tingling foot.

I'm waxing and waning in my dreams. Drunk on crepuscular cradle-sleep; the memory of a mother's rocking and cooing, and a green horse slinging itself through a tangerine sky.

Verdant foliage, sunshine stroking my face under a canopy of leaves. I bask in the warmth. Enrique and I have been walking in the garden when we make the discovery.

'We must look for the body,' I tell Enrique, as we stand together at the neck of the empty womb-tomb.

'Someone has stolen Him away,' I say. 'Naked,' I add, pointing at the fluttery, grave clothes lying on the stony ground.

People always think I'm stupid for stating the obvious. Enrique merely smiles.

'Let's look for the stone first, Paula,' he suggests, hand on my elbow, guiding me. We turn together, to chase a stone.

I'm wondering about that huge sacred stone. Not the body it sheltered, entombed or risen, but the stone itself, and how it came to be made that way: smooth, round, monolithic. Imagine a giant stone on the loose. As high as a man and thrice as wide. Smooth as an egg, round as an orange. Enrique and I are after that stone which does not want to be found. The stone is searching for a slope to make a quick escape.

'Look!' We both see it at the same time. The almighty stone is on the other side of the garden. It's moving away from us. The ground throbs with our pursuit; the stone picks up its pace. The race from the tomb! We're off. And so is the stone which has the Easter valley in its sights.

Enrique has taken my hand and we're running towards the renegade stone. We can't quite catch it. Now we're standing at the top of the hill, watching the stone rolling down a valley covered in sparkling ice. A crackling, cracking sound as the massive object shatters ice. We can't follow the stone down the hill. It's too steep and slippery. We don't dare.

At the bottom, the stone comes to a standstill, glows white and luminescent. The tombstone, an icy full moon. Enrique's hand turns to slush, loses its grip on mine. The cold is burning holes in my cheeks. I can't wake from the nightmare, as hard as I try. When the pain gets too much, my body decides for me.

I wake to the familiar winter sound of Prospera snapping kindling for the morning fire. I lift my cheek from the pillow and there she is, squatting in front of the hearth, cracking bits of wood between her strong, supple fists.

CHAPTER EIGHTEEN

The Return of Lost Belongings

In which Diego Velázquez visits the Morisco boy
Luis de Pareja a final time

'Oranges,' says Father Rastro, picking up his frothy glass.

'The first oranges of spring,' the servant nods, clearing away some bowls and utensils from an earlier meal. Rastro sniffs his juice as if it were a rose in bloom and drinks heartily. I'm looking at the orange pulp coating the inside of my glass. My top lip is wet, for in my excitement I've drunk too fast.

Luis has just told me an astonishing story, so after farewelling the lad in the courtyard, I requested an audience with Father Rastro to verify the news. He received me immediately and with much courtesy.

'So you will be going with them?' I inquire.

'I sought God's advice,' says Father Rastro, 'I believe it is the right thing to do.'

'The Council of the Inquisition would have objected,' I say.

Rastro shakes his head. 'They have agreed to let us go in the hope that we bring some Christians home to Spain.'

I don't like the sound of this. 'Are the Moriscos to be used as ransom?'

'Definitely not. The boys will be reunited with their families, if we can find them. It is a separate affair. In the meantime we have begun negotiations to exchange two Christian prisoners in Algiers, for two Muhammadan sailors we're holding in Málaga. One of the Mercedarian friars in Algiers is my older brother, Felipe Rastro.'

I nod. Luis has mentioned this imprisoned brother a number of times. The boys seem to think he's a glamorous individual for some reason, though I can't imagine why.

'When do you embark?'

'A week after Holy Sunday. We should arrive in Rabat by May.'

'And the Cordobans, Telmo and Arauz?'

'They will remain in the convento,' Father Rastro sounds pleased at this circumstance. 'It is their choice,' he adds.

'They would not wish to forfeit their weekly visits to Paula Sánchez,' I say with a smile, but immediately regret my audacity.

Rastro looks uneasy. He places his hands flat on the table and rises out of his chair. He turns, walks to the window and lifts the catch. Two startled pigeons buffet the pane of glass as they flutter away. Rastro opens the window wider and leans forward, so that his head is jutting out of the frame. From the courtyard below hammer blows resound and one of the builders bellows an instruction.

As Enrique Rastro takes in some air, I notice with satisfaction, that the Inquisition guards are no longer manning the surrounding roofs. On returning to Seville, Father Rastro showed a firm hand and ordered them off Mercedarian property. He examined the injured Moriscos, listened to the stories of their numerous escapes and for the first time — concerned about their physical safety — seriously considered their pleas for freedom.

Telmo and Arauz were allowed to visit Paula once a week, but they couldn't move in with her. Their request was not considered; neither the Castle nor the Church would approve of Morisco children residing with a former sinner, in a place of former (if not perpetual) sin.

Rastro is now attempting to close the window, his composure restored. Just as he's drawing the window shut, he reaches for a feather lodged on the sill between the latch and the frame. He discards the mottled plume, then secures the catch.

'He did not want me back in the convento,' was Paula's reedy lament to me when our paths crossed near the cathedral last week, 'but to make up for my exclusion, he let the boys come to me.'

Well, that may be the best solution. Love knows to fly direct. And he shies away, this priest.

'So, Master Velázquez,' Rastro says, 'I hope you will come down to the docks to wave us all goodbye.'

'Four Moriscos?' I query again.

'Four, yes. Luis, Benito, Remi and the young scholar, Camilo Contreras. He wants to find his family of origin too.'

The scholar priests, Rastro tells me in some amusement, didn't want to lose Camilo. They've been fighting to keep him in the seminary, but to no avail.

Father Rastro seats himself and asks me if I will also oblige. I sit, but a little uncomfortably; still rattled by the risks associated with the intended venture.

'It is the Mercedarian pledge,' he says, intuiting my thoughts.

'Your brother. Has he been a prisoner long?'

'He left Spain in 1600,' says Rastro. 'It was to have been

my first Holy assignment, but he went in my stead. We thought it would be a quick exchange, but all our attempts to return him have been unsuccessful. And Pope Paul has since discouraged our Mercedarian custom. His Holiness finds the sacrifice excessive.'

'Your brother went for you,' I repeat his words, conveying what I hope is my admiration. But I would do as much for my younger brothers, I suppose.

'My brother had been ransomed before and returned safely. I was young, only twenty-five, and feared the mission,' Rastro admits.

I sympathise. Or try to look sympathetic. Twenty-five sounds old to me, not young. And don't people get more cowardly with age? Not Father Rastro apparently.

'My mother would have wanted me to give Felipe his reprieve,' Rastro says then hesitates while he considers his empty glass. 'To take his place, if all else fails.'

So I see how it goes. If the planned exchange miscarries, Father Rastro will offer himself as a human ransom and let his long-suffering brother return. He seems resolved to pursue this plan. The outcome will decide the mission's merit. It may prove rash. Who could know beforehand?

I leave the convento, but not before I've promised to farewell Rastro and his charges on the docks next month. We will both be relieved of our guilt, somewhat, on that day. Luis de Pareja will get the chance to be reunited with his mother and sister, and Enrique Rastro with his long-lost brother.

I return home by a circuitous, contemplative route, finding myself in Catarina's street by chance. A Loyola sister appears ahead of me on the path, walking arm-in-arm with her mother. The daughter is veiled from head to toe like a Moor. The diaphanous veil swims around her as she walks. It might be a maid rather than one of the girls; the stature is too heavy for a Loyola sister. But I catch her eyes as she turns to enter the gate and I know they belong to Catarina. She looks at me but without recognition. No flirting, no interest. The urgency gone. The veil covering her nose and brow. If she has the pockmarks I wouldn't know.

The two women enter as one. The gate closes without either looking back and seeing my rude stare. I cross the street to buy some oil from a vendor. Keep an eye cocked on the house.

And the house keeps an eye on me. There's a snap of the gate and the smallest sister rushes across the street holding an urn in her arms. Is she coming for water? She stops in front of me.

Opens her mouth a couple of times like a fish, then speaks, 'She says sorry.'

This little girl, whose name I don't know, hands me

what she's holding. It's not an urn, as I imagined, but a cage with a dead bird inside. It's a goldfinch and it's probably mine. The cage I certainly recognise.

I take my belongings from the child but I don't know what to say. I look from the dead finch to the girl with her bird breast and beetle-bright hair.

'It went all quiet last night and died,' she whispers.

I haven't seen my bird for nine months so there's no surprise. Birds do have short lives. The feathers are still brilliant. Buff, yellow, red and white. The one eye I can see is shiny. Goldfinch, you once overflowed your cage; now you're just lying there spent. The little sister gives up waiting for me to say something. She shrugs and skitters away.

I walk home carrying my goldfinch cage in my left hand. Holding it still so that the bird doesn't knock about. When I'm back at Pacheco's I paint a likeness of my dead goldfinch, lying at the bottom of its cage in a pool of colours. I take out the bird, remove five feathers, one of each colour and arrange them in a narrow quill-holder. The weightless corpse I wrap in fine linen and bury in the garden beside the bones of the former loved Pacheco dogs. But I can't stop the feather lust. In the following weeks I go to the market and collect lots of dead birds that have expired in their cages. I carry them back to Pacheco's where I paint them on an old panel, one after another. Canaries, pigeons, rooks. The birds get bigger with each purchase; their inaction and silence get more terrible. The birds stay dead. The strings of their voices snapped. A double effacement of song and flight. Falling to death they fall so much further than we do when we die.

I'm remorseless. Hawks, roosters and a massive white swan with a long limp neck I harvest in my feather-lust. Until one day I come home with an ostrich that stinks out Pacheco's studio and makes him curse and retch. My master drags the putrid ostrich carcass outside and burns it on a pyre, and I stand there watching in dismay as the ostrich feathers pop out of its skin in the purple heat and blow away with the fan force of the fire. I know that some of these feathers land in the patios of San Vicente, for a few appear again in millinery splendour on my aunt's new hat in church the following Sunday.

The toll of beautiful, feathered dead and ruined love peters out, the ostrich ending my pillory of despair. Its head, its wrinkled neck would have been too human to paint, even if I'd got the chance.

Now comes the post-Lent fiesta as we speed round the bend of March into April and Marius Rosano is strutting across the square with a cornucopia on his head. He has bought a native headdress from the Americas. His mane is magnificent and he boldly struts, tossing his pagan tresses this way and that, 'Look at me, look at me.' I'd rather not. I nip behind the curtain of a bazaar. If Marius finds me in here I'm done for. But if I stay in the square he will eventually descend on me in all his finery. And he may tell me something I do not want to hear. He will tell me Catarina is scarred by the pox or he will tell me she is inviolate no longer. In this vain mood he's bound to hurt me. He will take something from me, he always does. Most friends do, but he more than most. I protect my girl in the blue cap from all that would harm and spoil her. I hold her close to my chest and wipe away the sweat the blue cap has made from rubbing against her brow.

CHAPTER NINETEEN

Overlooking the Guadalquivir River

She's been told the wrong time. Paula is knotting her hands together fretfully and saying 'Oh' repeatedly as if she's surprised and put out that she's missed the farewell on the docks.

There's a blur of boys running towards us and Telmo and Arauz bound up beside her. 'Sorry,' the brothers say, dragging on her shawled arms. 'That's the time we thought it was. But they woke us even earlier this morning.'

She might have been cross with Telmo and Arauz as it appears to have been their mistake, but their presence seems to cheer her up. They're standing on her feet as they muck around, ruining her pretty shawl as they swing on her from either side.

She's gone to a lot of trouble; she's looking very dressed up. I haven't seen that shawl before. It's embroidered with tiny pink rosebuds. And she's put up her hair. Her head is wrapped in a shiny scarf that's been wound around itself in the shape of a turban. The gold scarf is attracting a lot of sunlight. As I watch, the domed headdress connects with a needle of gold emanating from the summit of the watchtower rising behind her. Paula and the *Torre del Oro* are one.

I've no doubt that if Rastro was looking towards the dwindling party we have become on the docks, he would see the sun striking Paula's head like a beacon. The felucca bearing the Mercedarian party downstream is in the middle of the river now, cream sails fluttering, sailors drawing in their oars. I can see the Morisco boys standing on deck, still waving frantically at the shore. I'm absolutely sure which of them is Luis; he's always been the tallest boy.

I found it harder to say goodbye to him than I'd expected. I gave him a keepsake in parting, a silver pendant with a skull embossed on the metal. It's just the sort of amulet young boys love. Luis kissed the skull before he hung the chain around his neck. Then he kissed me on the cheek. That was embarrassing. I didn't like him doing that. He shouldn't have forgiven me yet, but he has.

The voyagers on the felucca are the size of fingers now. Soon they'll be too small to see. Other vessels are already blocking our view: tartans, barges and the frightening galleons. It's very busy on the river this morning.

Telmo and Arauz are pointing out Rastro's boat for Paula. They're still hanging onto her shawl. I step back from the water's edge. The crowd around us is thinning and I catch sight of Harmen's apprentice. 'Victor María!' I shout. I got to know this young man at Harmen's and Fillide's wedding. (Marius made sure I was sent an invitation.)

Victor María waves back at me and comes over to say hello. He's leading a donkey with a braided halter. Paula turns around to greet Victor María and we both remark on the presence of the animal in his company. Victor María explains that the beast has been carrying provisions for the voyagers — gifts from the Weddesteegs for Father Rastro on his long journey.

'Is Harmen Weddesteeg here too?' Paula inquires, looking around for him.

'He was,' Victor María assents, 'but his wife had a toothache.' Victor María laughs a bit recklessly at the memory of Doña Fillide's predicament.

'Too much marzipan apparently,' he continues, attempting to sound more concerned. 'She and Harmen left as soon as the boat did. I'm surprised you didn't spot them earlier.'

'I only just arrived. I missed everything.' Paula looks at the river in despair. The felucca is no longer visible. It's somewhere out there behind all the other boats.

'We could see them very clearly from the top of the Giralda,' I say to her. 'I could take you up there, if you'd like?'

Paula protests tiredness. 'Up the hill and then all those floors to climb,' she sighs.

Victor María offers the donkey's services for cathedral hill.

'You won't have to walk to the top of the tower either, Paula,' I insist. 'From halfway up there's a superb view.'

Paula says she's never ridden a donkey before, but as a girl she was always on and off her father's mule. Is the beast strong enough to carry her? She'll give it a try. Victor María holds the donkey and she manages to pull herself on lopsidedly. The donkey brays its objection.

'What a fool I must look,' she says, rearranging her skirt to cover her ankles.

'Not at all, not at all.' Victor María suppresses a smile.

We pass through the city gates and head uphill. I stride out in front while Victor María leads the donkey. Whenever I look back, Paula and Victor María are being passed on the road. When I get too far ahead, I stop. Let the others catch me up. Walking beside them, I hear Victor María say something to Paula about forbidden rocking horses and she laughs so much she slips off the donkey. This gives Victor María a chance to help her back on again.

At the entrance to the cathedral stable-yard I wait and watch while they secure the beast. They should stop laughing now, as we're going into the sacred citadel. I'm surprised at my own terseness, but they haven't included me in their joke.

'No visitors today. The bells are not ringing.'

'The bells, silent? For what reason?' We're standing at the Giralda gate.

'Maintenance. Some of the clappers are hanging loose.'

I'm about to turn on my heel, when Paula steps forward, opens her purse and hands the sacristan ten times the normal fee. She's getting into a party mood.

We are the only ones ascending, it seems. The walls echo our footsteps. Victor María and Paula have remained demure since entering the cathedral, so I stop resenting them.

'Have you been up here before?' Victor María eventually asks Paula.

'Never,' she whispers.

'You don't need to whisper,' Victor María replies.

'I can't help it.'

I'm counting the floors to the halfway mark. Twelve, thirteen, fourteen.

I loved doing this when I was a boy.

Paula has been keeping pace with us men. The climb doesn't seem to be troubling her.

'No bells to hurt your ears at the top, if you want to go all the way up,' I say to the others, encouragingly.

'No bells. Just like a mosque,' Victor María remarks.

'The ramp is so wide,' comments Paula.

She's right of course. There'd be room for a crowd of people to walk six abreast.

'So the Moors could ride up here on their mules,' I explain.

Soon afterwards we arrive halfway, at the sixteenth floor.

I let Paula and Victor María catch their breath while I jump up onto the ledge approaching the south-facing window. Below the Guadalquivir coils like a massive serpent, looping away in the distance. There are so many watercraft heading down the river today that I can't be sure which of the sailboats is carrying the Moriscos away from the city of their birth.

I hop down from the ledge so the others can take a look. Paula climbs up first, as there's not much space, and Victor María supports himself rather precariously behind her.

She seems rapt by the view.

'I can see the Church of El Salvador and the Town Hall and the Church of the Magdalena and even the Mercedarian convento,' she says with childlike wonder.

'But look to the river,' suggests Victor María.

Paula moves her head. She says nothing for a bit. 'Which is their boat, do you think?'

Victor María shakes his head. 'Your guess is as good as mine.'

I can't see Paula's face, but she sounds breathless rather than sad. Any disappointment took place earlier, on the dock. She wanted to say goodbye to Father Rastro, but perhaps he may not have wished to grant her such a civilised courtesy. The departure time had been changed to keep her away. I could tell from her anxious expression when she arrived at the water's edge that Paula was thinking of it as a reunion rather than as a farewell.

'I think I can see my house in Triana.' Paula is looking further afield.

'Can you see your house?' Victor María queries.

'Oh yes. On the rise, directly opposite the *Torre del Oro*. It's behind the one with the yellow flagpole.'

'Two storeys?'

'Two storey, yes. It has upstairs and downstairs,' Paula says, stating the obvious. She laughs at the silliness of her own remark. Victor María starts laughing too, warmly. He's laughing to keep her company, I realise.

I'm going to get nowhere with this pair today. They're acting like imbeciles. Why is Paula so friendly with Victor María? He's a pleasant enough man but he's practically a serf; she'd be paying for his services if it came to that.

Once again I try to persuade them to accompany me to the top of the Giralda, but Paula says she's too tired to go any further. She doesn't look tired, but I suppose she is.

I've never entered the tower without going all the way up to the minaret before. I owe it to myself to keep on climbing. For company I shout the numbers of the floors as I ascend. Thirty-one, thirty-two, thirty-three . . . Approach the final incline of steps where I lost my goldfinch. Climb up and up and out into the minaret with the white-frosted sun directly overhead. Take a walk around. See who else is up here. Not even one worker mending bells. A gritty, swirling wind is making my eyes water. I pull out a handkerchief and close my eyes to dab at them.

It isn't in my power to do it just yet, but in the future I intend to honour Luis and his friends and their families who've been driven from our land. A huge tableau is forming in my mind; a scene of weeping Moors flooding down cathedral hill, their battered baggage strewn along the gutters and a blind Christian beggar, caught up in the surge. In the bottom left-hand corner of the tableau is my unequivocal title, *The Flight of the Moriscos*, written in my large, sweeping hand. In the right-hand corner, my own name writ just as large.

I open my eyes, walk forward to the balcony and rest my lower body against the balustrade. Looking down I scan the flotillas on the Guadalquivir. Enough time has passed; I won't be able to find them down below, even if I had a telescope at hand. Enrique and the boys have turned the final bend in the river and sailed out of sight.

CHAPTER TWENTY

Paula Puts Her Lessons in Shared Balance to Good Use

On the sixteenth floor, Victor María and I sit side by side on the ledge in the half-light, holding hands.

'All those sittings in the convento . . .' I'm remembering with some regret.

'Yes?'

'You were there all along but I didn't notice,' I smile in disbelief.

'There was some competition.'

'No-one of significance,' I reply, then add ironically, 'except for the horse.'

'Rastro always chose his horses well,' Victor María speaks without enthusiasm.

'I sense you don't like him.'

'He pulled a nest of chicks out of a tree once. Surely you remember?'

'That's a good enough reason then,' I respond teasingly.

'So when did you first notice me?' Victor María asks.

I think I became aware of him when he turned up with the donkey on the dock this very morning. But now I know who he reminds me of.

'I dreamed you up, Victor María. There was a ladder-man who looked just like you; he was always around me, but I didn't make the connection.'

I've taken a risk saying this, and I await his response tentatively. Some men would find me a fibber or a fabricator.

'Ladder-men from the picaresques of Barbadillo?' he replies.

'I suppose so.' I've never heard of a writer called Barbadillo.

'And what did this ladder-man have to say for himself?' Victor María continues light-heartedly.

'Very little actually. He was mute.'

Victor María nods. 'Oh well, I hardly spoke to you in the convento, did I?'

'That's true,' I reply. It is only today that I've listened to and appreciated the sound of this young man's voice. Yet, if I had met him for the first time today, he would mean nothing to me. The months I spent in the convento, when I failed to hear him speak but was absorbing his essence anyway, have made this present attraction possible.

'So what did you two get up to if you couldn't talk?' Victor María presses.

I feel a little faint recalling an incident in the convento I'd completely forgotten. It happened during one of the early sittings. We'd stopped work for a spell and I'd embarked on a vigorous caprice. Victor María was helping me up onto the unsaddled white horse and I had once, twice perhaps, slid off the horse's smooth side. I had been trying to impress (amazingly, it seems to me now) Harmen Weddesteeg, prior to my feeling for Enrique Rastro arising. Victor María was no more than a faceless minor to me back then.

I lift a scrunched-up fist to Victor María's face and rest it against his cheekbone. I've found a word to describe his face. He's becoming. That's it. He leans forward and kisses me shyly and chastely on the mouth.

'We didn't get up to much,' I interrupt, eager to keep on talking rather than let Victor María bring my body back to life. The latter, being the most sought-after thing, is perhaps the most unbearable to countenance.

'The ladder-man taught me a lot of tricks of the trade,' I tell Victor María as he puts his arms around my waist and draws me closer.

This is what it means, I realise, when they say you wake up and find yourself a new person. I'm gulping air now, I'm gulping air lest hanging around his neck becomes lawful magic.

'Teach me his tricks then,' he says. Victor María, having unfisted me, has no fear.

But he doesn't really want to know. The art of falling into balance we've surely surpassed. And we have just this little bit of time to ourselves, to find out who we really are, before Diego returns.

POSTSCRIPT

In 1627, while living in Madrid, Diego Velázquez painted a large work, *The Expulsion of the Moriscos*, that won him a royal prize. Just over a hundred years later, in 1734, this painting was to be destroyed in the Madrid Alcázar palace fire, along with many other famous artworks.

References and Historical Sources for the Novel

The quotation on page vi is taken from Marcelin Defourneaux, *Daily Life in Spain in the Golden Age*, translated by Newton Branch (London: George Allen and Unwin Ltd, 1970) p 225.

Joaquin Hazanus y La Rua, *Vazquez de Leca, 1573-1649* (Seville: Sevilla Imprenta y Libreria de Sobrinos de Izquierdo, 1918) pp 254–6. (NB We know that some of the Seville orders were bringing up Morisco children who were left behind when their families went to Africa. Spanish documents cited in the above Seville publication, confirm that the children were distributed into the care of clergy and pious laymen.)

Mary Elizabeth Perry, *Gender and Disorder in Early Modern Seville* (Princeton: Princeton University Press, 1990).

Ruth Pike, *Aristocrats and Traders: Sevillian Society in the Sixteenth Century* (Ithaca & London: Cornell University Press, 1972) p 377. (NB Historical records indicate that in Seville three hundred children under seven were left behind by their families at the time of the great exodus which began in Seville in 1610.)

Velázquez in Seville, edited by David Davies and Enriqueta Harris (Edinburgh: National Gallery of Scotland, 1996). (NB The tower scene in the opening chapter of my novel was inspired by a historically documented incident. According to Vicente Canal, the inquisition notary Daza y Valdes took a group of male friends up the Giralda tower to test the range of a visorio (telescope). Daza, a close friend of Francisco Pacheco's, was familiar with Galileo's works. In 1613 Daza published *The Art and Use of Telescopes*, a text in which, according to Vicente Canal, Daza recounts the ascent of the Giralda episode. See Vicente Lleo Canal, 'The Cultural Elite of Velázquez's Seville', in *Velázquez in Seville* referenced above, pp 26–27.)

Acknowledgements

Thanks to those who have offered support, encouragement and editorial advice on the novel over the seven years that it has been in the making.

Professor Jane Arnold of Seville University was endlessly helpful when I visited Spain in 2003 to research the novel. More recently she has read the manuscript and assisted with the Spanish language and other textual matters. Thanks to Jenny Lee, Clara Tuite, Gail Jones, Wendy Faris and Virginia Maxwell for appraising the manuscript in its early stages. A big thank you to London literary agent Laura Morris for her time, enthusiasm and useful editorial advice.

A special thanks to everyone at HarperCollins, in particular Linda Funnell for her patience and for her thorough and astute editing. Thanks to freelancer Belinda Lee for her thoughtful copyedit, and also to Jo Butler.

Finally to my family, who, though reluctant readers of my writing, when badgered by me have helped out by reading little samples. I could not have done without your presence and your continued belief in me and in the value of writing.